Headwaters

Headwaters

a novel

MICHELLE MORACZEWSKI

Headwaters is a work of fiction. Names, characters, places, and incidences either are the product of the author's imagination or are used fictitiously. Any resemblance to actual persons, living or dead, events, locales is entirely coincidental.

Homestead Productions
First Draft, 2015

ISBN 978-0986149641

Illustrations by Michelle Moraczewski
Book Designed by Carianne Lance

Printed in the United States of America

For my Father, the storyteller in my life.

"His land is big and vast and he honors the land of his birth, by traveling upon it, living with it, from it and on it."

*"You must speak straight so your words
may go as sunlight to our hearts."*

Cochise, Chiricahua, Apache

CHAPTER 1 *Water*

The last car crunched stones as it splashed through the stream. The last bang sounded as the cattle gate shut. After all the people, laughter, and flying hammers, The Ranch was silent.

The spring oozed forth water from beneath the earth's surface and sparkled in the brilliant sunlight, flooding through moss and ferns. Endless waterways etched sharp trails in the face of the limestone cliff, and then flowed forth on the wide, shallow riverbed. Thousands of years ago, this had been a mighty river. Now the river was a slip over a smooth limestone floor with only a few feet of water and a slippery coat of algae on the bottom in a wide gulf between two cliffs. Millions of years ago it had been an ocean. This was the Edwards Plateau.

> *"How do you talk about something as familiar as a lover that you see every day? You know their face, even in the dark or with your eyes closed. You feel the hot breath. You know their smell. And then it's gone— torn from you forever. Something so common and daily, loved with all the familiarity as if it's a part of you. The beat the heart beats as if it's in you. Already a part and held deep within." - Mariah's Journal*

Texas—hot, hidden, elusive—with bone deep beauty. Yes, the usual rocks, cliffs, scrubby trees, and sugar maples. Sticky suggestive sweet smells with water clear as glass and a horizon all the way to the earth's curve. Shimmering polished pebbles in ice water streams. Small black balls and sea green algae, bone-dry heat, scorpions, butterflies, prickly rough cedars, endless Freda Kahlo painted blue sky, straw long grasses, crickets, frogs, hawks, ravens, and goats. Forgotten homesteads, solid rock chimneys with spindly cedar fences, and cactus flower color. Wind whipped up from the ribbon river valley and through red rock canyon walls.

A hawk flew around and around circling the landscape. The spring gushed forth, its pearl drops sparkled brighter than diamonds and far more precious in the dry Texas landscape. The water ran half a mile before filling a lake full of rainbow-colored fish. The wind blew; the maples around the lake rustled with a tambourine-like jingle. Bats hid in the cave at the cliff bottom. A nut disappeared into the river as it rushed to join the Nueces, on the journey to the sea. Water sped from the south fork until it joined the branch coming from the Blue Spring and formed the river. A doe stood calmly by the water, quenching her thirst.

The water flowed by the empty silent house, locked up again for who knows how long. The water flowed through the property for ten miles before it left, joined by other forks to form the Nueces River. The hawk above rode the current in the hundred-degree Texas heat. Water: more precious than anything. Eyes watched.

To tell this tale, will we start at the beginning? Or, after what Mariah would later refer to in her journal as, "that one event, the singular occurrence that woke us all up, that shocked us, and would change us forever?" It was like asking when to begin telling the story of the Garden of Eden—was it during those long, perfect idyllic days of bliss? Or after evil had invaded, tainting everything in its path? The wake-up call: perverting the continuous cycle of birth - death – rebirth. Death in the form of murder is a crime against both man and Nature. It is against the Divine order of things.

Perhaps it is like Pandora's box. Or the person you took for granted, with whom you thought you could indulge your whims and slippery sidetracks, only to find them suddenly gone, leaving nothing in their place. Nada. It is too late and you cannot go back. For Mariah, that was the Texas she used to know, the Texas that had been torn from her forever, leaving her forever never whole

CHAPTER 2 *David Agnelli*

Mariah sat on the floor of the warehouse, tugging on her running shoes. Spring found Mariah longing for the Texas she used to know. The place she had grown to love. Time had flown since that week at The Ranch, consumed by the usual day-to-day of teenagers who had turned from high school to college, with all focus on the Future with a capital 'F.' It had been seven years.

Was it fate or accident that brought two people with divergent paths together? They had backed into each other in the crowded urbanity of Houston, Texas. And now...

"David?" Mariah's voice echoed in the cavernous space. The warehouse that David Agnelli used as an art studio was massive. The space was raw brick with frosted steel windows that let light in, but wouldn't let her see out. Consequently, Mariah forgot they were in the heart of downtown. This place was cool, and David was the coolest artist she'd ever met. The space was large, three thousand square feet of industrial space. David created sculptures as well as large, wall-sized paintings.

He emerged from the makeshift bathroom, which he had installed; complete with a claw-foot tub, which he had found. The shower curtain hung from a plumbing pipe and the white PVC was exposed.

"I had to brush my teeth before we left," he smiled, flashing his pearly whites at her.

Mariah returned his grin. "Are you ready to go now?"

David's eyes, an impossible aquamarine, held hers, his serious, steady gaze a contrast to his playful demeanor. David Agnelli was not one to be taken lightly; he may seem the southern gentleman, but his calm good manners masked an intense, almost Latin passion just below the surface. Mariah guessed that was what made him so creative and productive at his work.

They had first met at an art gallery. No surprise there, Houston was full of them. Their first date lasted six hours as they shut down galleries, restaurants, and finally, Watson's Bar in Houston's Old Quarter before he drove her home and kissed her on the doorstep. There would be many incredible escapades in the Houston night scene, but after that first night, she knew. It was get out now or play for keeps. Wasn't much of a decision, not with the way he held her, like he would never let go. Mariah liked that. She liked some things not being up for debate. She was his and he was hers.

Damn good-looking, too, she thought, as she watched him push his brown curly locks out of his eyes as he approached a painting. He made a last-minute scribble with a large dirty brush he grabbed from the can of turpentine.

"David, do you know where I'd like to go on our honeymoon?"

David watched as Mariah struggled and tugged with the sneaker, one tan leg stuck out straight, until it finally slipped onto her foot.

She quickly laced them up. "I'd like to go to the Ranch."

"Sure," he said. "Anywhere you like."

"Are we going to the art opening tonight after our run?"

Art opening, shmart opening," he mimed. "Where is it this time?"

"You know, in the Museum District on Bisonette. Near Rice."

"Well, maybe. I still have work to do to be ready for my show."

"Yeah. I kind of want to go."

The two piled into his pickup for the quick trip down Memorial Drive to the park. David tuned the radio to the Pacifica rock station and the English Beat blared.

"What's The Ranch anyway?" He asked after a few minutes. "I didn't know you had a ranch."

She paused for a beat, surprised that she'd never told him about

The Ranch. Sometimes she forgot they hadn't known each other all that long. "I don't exactly have a ranch; it's more like access to one. It belongs to my dad's friend, Peter." She sat up straighter in her seat and watched Houston's car lots and fast food joints pass by out the window. "It's a very special place. Special to me, anyway."

The park was crowded. David and Mariah stood by the entrance to stretch. "The Ranch is," her voice caught, "great," she said, as she twisted to her left. "My dad has been taking me there since I was sixteen. Haven't been there in a long while, what with work and traveling around the world meeting interesting guys ..." She grinned at him and they headed toward the track and went into a slow jog. Mariah glanced at David, gauging his mood. She panted as they picked up the pace. "Go on, I know you run faster than I do. I'll tell you about The Ranch later."

She didn't have to say it twice. David pulled ahead of her, trying to dispel the stress of his upcoming show. Mariah was grateful for the chance to observe her surroundings. The park was energized with Houston's after-work joggers, running, walking, and panting by. She'd watched them pull up in shiny Jaguars and Porsches, emerging with glistening tanned bodies. Some of the men were perfumed for the nightclubs they frequented much later.

The rhythmic meter of her jog sent her right back to her first encounter with The Ranch. She'd been only sixteen...

Mariah had surveyed the bone-white boulders that studded the shallow stream before her. Her dad's Malibu hadn't quite made it over the last river crossing, so she was on foot in the Texas heat to get help. She was sure she could make it across. She backed up a few steps for momentum, and then took off dancing across the stream from rock to rock. On her last leap to the edge, she slipped, and with one soggy tennis shoe, she climbed the bank.

Her dad's idea of fun was to drag Mariah and her seven younger siblings on a day-long drive in a hot car to an isolated cabin in the middle of nowhere. She saw the stone house, just past the boughs of sugar maples angled at the edge of a low bluff. She breathed in deep, enjoying the sticky-sweet smell and the sound of burnt grass crunching like straw under her feet as she headed toward the driveway. Faint voices emanated from the house, growing louder as she reached the screen door. She had just raised her hand to knock when the door swung open to reveal a tall man smiling down at her. From behind him the sound of laughter bespoke a party in midstream, and Mariah realized that she stood there a total stranger, an unknown emissary for her dad. One half of her was hot and dirty, the other half wet, and she was sure her dark hair was a mess. A gust of dry wind whipped her hair in her face, blinding her for a moment.

"Hi," she said, returning his smile. "You must be Peter? I—we—my dad—Steven French ..." Hair stuck to her mouth as she continued. "We've driven all the way from Houston and ..."

"Hi!" Peter said and opened the door wide. "Come on in, we're just visiting. Have a beer? Do you know Fanny and Matt?"

Mariah glanced past him into the crowded kitchen, then down at her wet mess of an outfit. "Dad got the Malibu stuck on the third river crossing," she said. "I came ahead to get help."

"I see," Peter said. He set his beer down on the side table by the door. "Not a problem, I'll grab some of the guys. You go on in, make yourself at home." Peter stepped out onto the porch.

"Thanks," Mariah said, relieved. She hated asking for help.

Peter called back through the screen door. "Steven is here; he's stuck!"

Matt Weston stood with the other men, all in knit shirts and shorts with beers in hand. Mariah knew Matt. He was one of her dad's best friends.

"I'll grab a jeep," Peter said. "I'll probably need some help pulling them out." He took big strides to the shed where all the jeeps and four-wheelers were parked.

Fanny and the other women, their slender fingers holding chilled wine in long-stemmed glasses, poked their heads into the kitchen

15

to check out the fuss. Mariah looked at their white jeans topped with orange and pink silk tanks and lowered her eyes. Her tennis shoes were not just wet, she realized, they were downright filthy.

A moment later, Peter pulled the jeep around to the front of the house.

Mariah turned toward him. "I'll come with you," she called. "I'll show you where we got stuck."

"Sure," he said, chuckling. Peter was just as easygoing as her dad had described him.

Mariah stepped off the porch and looked out at the endless horizon. The big Texas sky, like a presence, dominated the land. She knew they were deep in the middle of nowhere. This was forgotten territory. Peter extended a large freckled hand and pulled her up into the seat beside him. Mariah blushed.

"There are eight of us, plus my dad. Did he tell you?" Her voice was weak. "I'm sorry to interrupt your party."

Matt hopped into the back seat. "It's okay, girl," he said, slapping Peter on the shoulder. "Peter is used to it. Not all his friends drive pickups or jeeps."

In no time they had bumped back down the gravel road and over the stream. Around the bend they heard the engine revving as Steven tried to budge the car. They drove up and pulled to a stop.

Spewed dust hovered around the turquoise Malibu like a smoke cloud. Mariah saw the wide-eyed faces of her siblings as they peered out of the dark windows like frightened deer. With a pang, she realized she'd been gone more than an hour. She got out and ran to the car.

"Peter's come to help us!"

Steven French emerged from behind the wheel and clasped Peter's hand. "Great to see you, Peter, thanks for coming to the rescue. Would you like a beer?" No matter the circumstances, Steven French always managed to have a cooler on hand loaded with ice water, cold beer, sharp cheddar, and salami—All that plus plenty of 35mm film.

Steven French was a photographer. Like most members of his profession, he considered it more of a calling than a job, which meant he was always, and yet never, working. He always wore his camera around his neck. On weekends he took candid shots of his friends, and later presented them with handsome black-and-white prints. He had serious jobs—with commissions, deadlines, and demanding clients, many of which were art galleries. He'd shoot the gallery opening, lavish, yet tasteful affairs where the colorful art crowd mixed with the somber Houston elite. Much of the city's art scene in the 1970's and 1980's had been captured on black and white film thanks to Steven French and his Nikon.

CHAPTER 3 *Sisters*

Mariah sprinted into the present moment and caught up with David. The two ran side by side in companionable silence, each lost in thought.

It had been more than a while since Mariah had been to The Ranch; in fact, it had been years. She managed frequent visits while in college, but afterward she had been busy traveling in Europe and establishing a serious career. Now, she was back in Texas. Seeing all her brothers and sisters again brought back many good memories, especially those of The Ranch. She and Kristen were inseparable back then. The sweaty Houston humidity was miserable, unlike the Ranch's dry heat.

As a sun goddess, she couldn't get enough sun back then. She remembered, the sun blazed down from on high, on the endless lazy days. The three sisters, Kristen, Mariah, and Kate, wandered through the woods and swam all day in the springs. Sunbathing on an incredible quiet, humming day was marvelously relaxing. Mariah sprinkled water lazily on her tan belly to keep cool.

In the distance, she heard hammers fly and a few voices high in the clear air as volunteer crews worked on the schoolhouse. The women helped their husbands or hung out together in the shade. No one seemed to notice Kate, Kristen, and Mariah as the only teenagers, or care what they did, thus they had free rein to escape to the river.

"I feel unbelievably free out here. It's like another world. It's as if the rigid rules for worldly existence don't apply," Mariah said.

"Aren't you tired of just lying there?" Kristen asked.

"No. I'm not just lying here, I'm working on my tan."

Kristen nodded, "Let's run down to the Indian paintings."

"OK, that's a great idea." Mariah closed her book. She hadn't gotten in much reading on this trip.

The two girls left Kate with her camera and took off. Kristen's favorite pastime was to abandon Kate. She'd learned long ago to entertain herself if she wasn't interested in the chase, only lately focusing on photography, and assisting their dad in the dark room.

Kristen swiped Kate's sun-hat as they took off.

"Hey," Kate yelled.

But they were gone to jump boulders in the semi-dry riverbed below the canyon. A scant ribbon of water was left at the wide canyon bottom, where one could walk along the face of the wall. Peter's friends usually did. They were all grown-ups, seriously attired, tripping like pioneers in heavy boots and wide-brimmed hats to protect overly white skin. Kristen and Mariah knew the others were far away at the schoolhouse and they were utterly alone.

Large boulders, at least six to eight feet wide chunks of rock, lay at the bottom of the deep ravine. The gouge in the earth was about sixty feet or more. With cliffs shooting straight up on both sides, it felt narrow. When around water, Kristen and Mariah's favorite way to travel was barefoot. Dressed in short cutoffs and bathing suit tops to capture a great tan while playing in this giant jungle gym, they lost track of time. They climbed to the top of each boulder and jumped to the next, scrambling for the best foothold as they negotiated the path through the riverbed. Mariah marveled at the small trees, vines, and grasses that managed to grow through the cracks in the stones. It was neither dangerous nor difficult, but it was fun. Her focus was on nothing but the pure physical act of enduring hot stones on bare feet. It felt like flight as she jumped and leaped from stone to stone. Her sister, Kristen, was a challenge to hike with, as she was taller, braver, and leaner. Left behind, Kate had her camera, and her sisters knew she was serious about following in their father's footsteps. It was a rare opportunity for Mariah and Kristen to slip off by themselves.

"Hey, no one's out here," Kristen said. "Let's take our tops off. That way we can get a real tan."

"Easy for you to say, you won't bounce."

"Chicken." She splashed Mariah.

"At least I don't look like one," Mariah muttered.

"I don't see anyone out here for miles. No one's coming. Everyone's busy back at the schoolhouse. If anyone decides to come we'd see them from far off," Kristen said.

"All right." Mariah struggled with the clasp as she removed her green and yellow bathing-suit top. She tied it to her shorts making her hands free for climbing. The sun felt hot on her back. She wet her hair in the stream and smoothed it back with her hands. "I feel weird, kind of naked and free."

"You'll get used to it," Kristen said knowingly. The two sisters splashed through the water. "Wait, we're only halfway there, we have a ways to go yet."

"Look," Kristen pointed. There was a wall of water, springs etching their way down through the limestone wall to the river. The sharp ridges dug into Mariah's feet as she hiked up the thirty feet to the source. Water spilled from the fern and moss-hidden stream. She switched to the soft piles of lime green moss that lined the edges of the rivulets of water. Cold water tickled her bare feet beneath the fern and moss. When they reached the source, they drank their fill from the fresh springs. "I guess this used to be a waterfall. Now it's a continuous flow making a wall of water, even in this drought," Mariah said.

The two cupped their hands and drank the sweet water. "How far are those cave paintings?" Mariah asked.

"Way down there. We'll recognize them when we get close. They're on the other side."

"Let's do it." They resumed hiking, long hair bouncing on backs and tops tied to their shorts. "I've turned native," Mariah said. "It's liberating. Glad Mom's not here."

"Me, too. You would never do it if she was."

"Right," Mariah said.

The two focused on their steps. Mariah marveled at what a free spirit Kristen was. She was athletic, daring, and popular. She had tons of guy friends because she was a tomboy. At home, she did all the outdoor chores: mowed the lawn, clipped the hedges, she even washed the family car. Mariah had to stay in the house, and cook, clean, and nurture the little ones.

Weekdays at home were filled with school and homework. Saturday was filled with chores and cleaning all day long. Sunday was half gone by the time they finished church and brunch. Her only free time was a window of opportunity on Sunday afternoon. She had gotten into the habit of leaving, in order to get anything done. It seemed she was always in search of private airspace to think her thoughts all the way through. But here, she stared up at the endless blue sky. She felt free, as if she could just keep walking and never turn back.

"Hey," Kristen shouted. "Look, there it is!" She thrust her slender arm out, finger pointed. They looked off to the distance and saw the dark slash in the cliff on the opposite bank. Mariah squinted. Yes, there was clearly a cave in the cliff face.

The cave's indentation off in the distance wasn't all the way up. She let her feet dangle from a rock in a deep spot of the river as she studied the cliff. It shouldn't be too hard to scale. May as well wade to the other side, she thought. Once across, Kristen was ahead, of course. "C'mon," she yelled.

"I'm just cooling off before we climb up. It looks hot on that rock wall," Mariah said.

"Excuses. The cave is shady." Kristen was eager to climb.

"I guess." Mariah squinted up.

The teens scaled the cliff face. About twenty feet up they arrived. The cave was a roomy hollowed-out space open to the sky. They walked around freely kicking at the remains of a campfire. A projecting rock ceiling shaded the ledge, and the girls paused for a moment to put their tops back on. There were smoke stains on the wall beside a huge painted mural. Peter, they knew, camped with his buddies all over the property.

The burnt-orange Indian mural, almost 6 feet tall, depicted stick figures, deer, and various animals. Kristen inspected the wall. "Look. It's signed C.H.G. 1887." Underneath, there were worn names and dates that were difficult to read. "Looks like 1919, I think. These marks have been here a long time."

The marks were painted an iron oxide red. There were cattle or buffalo and other signs and symbols. "It's a whole language we don't know. What could it mean?"

Kristen glanced over at Mariah. "How long ago were these images painted? Do you think this was an Indian dwelling?"

Mariah shrugged. "Looks that way. We should ask Peter. If anyone knows the history of this place it would be him."

Mariah sat cross-legged on the dirt floor and contemplated the figures on the wall. Sharp bits of shell dug into her palms as she leaned back on her arms, but she barely noticed, she stared intently searching for meaning in these foreign hieroglyphics.

"You look like you're waiting for them to speak to you," Kristen prodded.

"I do wonder how old they are. Primitive cave drawings, I suspect. I think the river might have run right by here long ago. I guess it's etched its way down over the years."

Mariah stared at the huge expanse of blue sky above the cliff. Could that be a figure peering over the edge? No it must just be a plant. "No one else is out here right?"

"Hey, what's up there?" Kristen called. The two girls glanced up at the cactus pear plant above them.

"Are you trying to scare me?"

"I thought I saw something move. Let's check it out."

"Don't go. What if it's not just a plant?"

"Are you crazy? We should catch them. I'm going to the top!" Kristen exclaimed.

Mariah's curiosity overcame her trepidation. The climb looked daunting, but she scrambled up to follow. After a few scratches, pulling each other up, they climbed over the edge. Now at the top, they stood and walked around, speechless. The three-hundred-sixty-degree view spanned a great distance. The land was as flat as an ocean as far as the eye could see. The sun was a large hazy glow, masked by low cloud cover. It was still a couple of fists above the horizon.

"Wow," Kristen's voice was hushed, her tone reverent.

"Yeah," Mariah whispered in awe, "flat, like Texas. I guess we're on top of the Edwards Plateau."

They looked down from their perch at the boulder-strewn canyon. "We were like ants down there. The scale is amazing." Kristen's breath caught.

"We're kind of alone in the middle of it." Mariah spread her arms wide and spun around in a circle until she was dizzy. "We have it all to ourselves. It feels like freedom."

Kristen stared at her and then laughing, joined in. The two of them laughed and danced, drunk on the wide-open space. They sang the duets they knew from childhood, two voices melded together like one smooth tone. They held hands and spun around in a circle, singing louder and louder. They each drew energy from the other.

"You know," Kristen said after starting to sober up, "I saw something peering over the edge as I was climbing up. I'm not making that up."

"Did it seem like a figure dressed in buffalo skins? Long dark hair?" Mariah asked. "I'm kidding," she laughed.

"I'm not," Kristen said. "I saw what looked like a figure in the distance moving away. Then it was gone. With all this emptiness up here there is no place to hide."

"Exactly. No place to hide." Mariah went along. Her sister had a great imagination. "It must have been the cactus pear plant we saw after all."

Kristen shivered. "We have to get back. We don't want to be out here after dark." She clutched her stomach. "Besides, I'm hungry."

"You're always hungry." Mariah peered hard into the distance, watching for shapes in the larger clumps of cacti. "But you've lasted this long, you can last a little longer." She couldn't see anything but flat land and endless sky. The haze of clouds cleared and the sun angled orange rays, making the straw grass glow and cacti etched in haloes. Mariah giggled at the childishness of it all.

* * *

The Ranch—site of her favorite adventures with her siblings. It was lost to her for a time in the whirlwind of art and architecture… and David. She had fallen backward into love with him, literally. She was freshly back from studying art in Paris at an atelier and putting a résumé together for a hoped-for career in New York City when they met. She had been engaged to a Texas cowboy, a country singer, who thought a move to New York would betray his Southern code. That abruptly ended when she met David. They were a team.

CHAPTER 4 *Art*

One evening Mariah had been out with her artsy friends, checking out a series of gallery openings. While standing before a painting, she took a few steps back literally into the tall strong back of a stranger.

"Hello again," said David, when she turned to apologize. It was the third gallery they had run into each other.

"I know you," Mariah said. "We met last year. You had some sculptures in the Bayou show. Are you showing here tonight too?"

Next thing you know he had invited her to his one-man show at a contemporary art gallery on the East Coast. This was very impressive to someone who lived in a city crawling with experimental artists all showing *somewhere* around town. Since she'd never had a serious art exhibit in her life, despite her education and intense passion, she was deeply captivated.

Mariah laughed politely, then steered the conversation away from the invitation. She had never heard that line before. Whatever the case, she ditched her girlfriends and followed the handsome guy to several more galleries before taking the conversation to the *'oldest bar in town'* in Houston's Old Quarter—Watson's. As she listened to this young southern artist, his master's degree still wet under his arm, talk about his shows at Houston's Contemporary Art Museum and other prominent galleries, she couldn't hide her admiration—or was it envy? How amazing his paintings must be to have a second show on the East Coast.

"The first one," he said, "had been a group show, with three painters, but this would be a solo."

On the other hand, having shows didn't mean one was necessarily a good artist, just one with connections. As he spoke about his life, she couldn't help wondering, was he a terrible nihilist of an artist with dark paintings? Or an artistic genius? What if after enjoying his company, she found out he was a really bad painter? He explained that every single thing he'd painted all year had been packed and shipped out to the gallery. He was living in an empty warehouse space in downtown Houston. A living/studio; completely empty. Her mind worked furiously. She had just spent eight months in Europe. Her eyes were adept at viewing art. His show was scheduled to open in three weeks, and when he asked again if she would come, she could no longer deny that she was tempted. The thing was, should she jeopardize her three-year engagement to Justin to do it?

Given this tall, extremely genteel, blue-eyed guy was offering the only way she could see his etchings was with a trip to her favorite part of the country, she couldn't just turn it down. "Hmm... I don't know. We've seen each other around town, but I don't really know you." She actually didn't know how to drive a car, but she knew how to board a plane. Thus a trip to the East Coast was plausible.

"Well then, let's get to know each other," had been his response. Thus they had spent the next week going out every single night. At the time, her fiancé was on the road somewhere.

Wednesday Mariah went to work as usual. After the night they had, she expected his call. He said that his art professor, Julian Marcus, was in town and a group of U. of H. buddies would all go out for Mexican probably. When Mariah arrived home after another boring day at the grindstone, grinding out beach house floor plans after the hurricane-damaged Galveston, her roommate, Kurt, was monopolizing the phone.

Her sister Kate greeted her, "David called. You should call him pronto if you're interested in joining a big group out for Mexican food."

Finally, Mariah wrangled the phone from Kurt. He'd been wandering around the house with his shirt off, displaying an artful chest of tattoos, his long black hair tangling in the chord as he yakked away in his New Jersey accent.

She liked Kurt because he played in a rock band. What had she been thinking subletting a room to him? The economic reality of the single life in a big town.

* * *

When she called David, she caught him just in time. He soon swung by in his white pickup. By the end of the week he was picking her up straight from work. He invited her on a trip to see Axel Mane, David's sculpture teacher's huge show of mega-sculptures in a contemporary Dallas gallery. All his artist buds were carpooling and driving up *en mass*. It seemed David had somewhere important or fun to be every day of the week.

It was a whirlwind courtship: movies—Phillip Glass; dinners—Mexican or Italian; poetry readings at the MFA; and a seemingly endless list of art openings and studio tours. After they had spent a day driving to Dallas for Axel Mane's huge Texas show—that was it. They had officially "gotten to know one another." Time to buy a plane ticket and go. Let come what may...

The New York art scene was all over Soho with Mary Boon, Leo Costelli and Paula Cooper Gallery showcasing the Neo-Expressionists of the day. Soho was a ghost town of huge warehouses with big rambling elevators that worked just as well for the mega-pieces of contemporary art as the industrial baggage they were originally made for. When the two returned from New York together, it was late and David suggested Mariah stay over in his art studio/warehouse. By now they had spent every night together for the past ten days, sleeping on friends futons from Philadelphia to New York.

Mariah lay in David's loft bed, fitted tight to the ceiling, in the warehouse he called home. She could see morning light through the rips in the metal roof. The loft was sized for a futon and a bunch of down comforters and pillows. She felt at home, perhaps because she was with him.

Light from frosted steel windows streamed into the warehouse. As her eyes accustomed to her surroundings, she noticed plastic sheeting duct-taped to the ceiling formed a sort of funnel below the skylight. A row of healthy green plants grew in a frenzy spilling out of their pots. Some ivy grew down the shelf draping itself around the makeshift kitchen.

Come what may, had led to this. Now there was a wedding to be planned. Dates, arrangements and reality were moving so fast that this train would be at the station in a week. Thoughts of family naturally lead to thoughts of The Ranch. And now she was inviting him to her favorite place on God's whole green earth.

As a sought after artist, David had three 6' x 7' paintings going simultaneously. He also had a new sculpture commission to complete. Mariah made coffee in an Italian stove top espresso maker. After a breakfast of bagels and scrambled eggs, David invited Mariah to join him on a scavenger hunt. They drove through the strange Houston junk yards in the sort of industrial wasteland of downtown. There were piles of industrial castoffs that were there for a smile and a person with a pickup truck. It was fun to run around town collecting junk for his *found object* sculpture. The current piece, *Wedge Mobile Fortress*, was a self-contained escape vehicle—designed for lone survival. A one-man vehicle—fortress against the world—complete with canned goods, a hot plate, and a propeller. Although Mariah doubted it would ever get off the ground. She watched in horror as David pounded used barn wood and rusted metal all over the exterior of his *Wedge*. He found 2 x 4's and bamboo and rescued wood with the nails still in it to form the large piece. It was 10' long and 6' tall in places. Art structures were quite different from the pristine modernism Mariah had been doing while in New York.

She went back to her small corner of his expansive studio. Her oil painting, small in comparison, sat on an easel. She was working on a series about Greece. Each of her tiny brushes were wiped clean. Her oils were laid out by color on a glass palette. He had convinced her to quit her job and hang out full-time with him painting in his studio on those long spring afternoons.

'Fresh Paint' was the huge deal all of the local artists were preparing for. For the first time ever, local artists would be chosen for a show at the Museum of Fine Arts Houston. Thanks to an open-minded museum director, the Houston grass-roots art movement was going mainstream. David's paintings were certainly fresh and wet. Expressive about what he believed in—plants marching on the city; glass office towers overtaken by kudzu; slender elegant forms of an oil refinery with the plumes of smoke becoming blackbirds in a stormy sky—a metamorphosis of hope. He'd found art in a place all her life she'd wanted to escape. In contrast, her paintings were escapes into white stucco forms against pure blue Mediterranean skies and islands floating in a calm cold sea. Opposites attract.

They painted all day, went for runs at the park, and frequented art parties at night. One afternoon, after a run, Mariah sat on an old van seat used as a couch, downing ice water. The skylight lit up another of David's paintings. Still in shorts, hot and sweaty she studied the large piece, a guy clutching a palm tree by a raging sea. The tree bent sideways by the wind, his body thrown horizontal in sheer determination to hold on. Although a disaster painting, the balance of composition and intensity of the marks made it a beautiful piece. After his shower, David came back in and continued to work. Mariah found the spectacle fascinating. She lay back, did her leg stretches, while she watched him work.

She realized she had calmed down a lot since her last trip to

Europe. Going to the middle of nowhere with the guy she loved seemed the most sincere commitment to the life she wanted to lead with him.

CHAPTER 5 *Houston*

Mariah hummed as she prepared a meal for herself and her fiancé in the makeshift kitchen of his cavernous, three-thousand-square-foot warehouse. They had gotten in the habit of having dinner together after a day in the studio, usually followed by an art exhibit or a film at the River Oaks Theater. Although she knew it was healthy to be a vegetarian, she couldn't give up meat entirely; they ate a lot of vegetarian meals. Today it was green beans from the farmers market, slow-cooked in a crock-pot with basmati rice. She painstakingly shucked them and pulled the strings.

They had both been painting in David's studio all day. David's large paintings were stapled to the walls. Today had been extremely productive. He was preparing for 'Fresh Paint.' By now the Houston art scene had become a movement with a certain distinct style emerging. The Museum of Fine Arts and the Contemporary Art Museum could no longer ignore this. Mariah was not a part of it, as her realistic style was in complete contrast to David's exuberant expressionistic one.

She wore roller-skates in the loft while she cooked, a habit begun while in university. They came in handy now. She rolled around the concrete floors of David's place. Roll to observe a painting, then glide back to the kitchen or to her own work. She officially still lived at her dad's house a few blocks away, with a few of her sisters. She kept her things at David's.

The art studio building was a warehouse on Chenevert Street, a few empty blocks from the huge skyscrapers that made up downtown Houston proper. There were few cars on this edge of downtown at night; Houston at night became a ghost town. After dinner David abruptly left the table, and jumped back into painting without a word. Mariah piled the dishes into the sink and stood there. It was a humid summer night. She felt itchy and sticky. She realized she felt trapped.

She opened the door into the dark night. She skated through the quiet streets to Main Street, then skated down Main ten blocks to Market Square. She had no thought but to run. Run away as fast as she could. Her mind raced. What to do? All sense escaped as she sped to catch her thoughts.

She kept moving. Pushing, rolling to the parking garages everyone used, as they were vacant at night. The noise echoed all around as she wound down the smooth slick ramp, round and round for several floors. She was hot and sweaty with effort. Now what? She raced back to Market Square, grateful for the wind's cooling affect. She must think through this. She found a bench and plopped down.

David had asked her to marry him. She'd agreed. Now they were playing house. She could see her future flash before her eyes. Romance dies, she's left making dinner and doing dishes the rest of her life as his art matters more. His work will be in the Big Show. Not hers. She knew consciously, she didn't fit in here in Houston. She was proud of his success, really. She just wanted her own important work as well. Even the gallery director implied that she would be called upon to support him financially, so he could devote his life to his art. That is what an Art wife does. She began to skate and fume. She had to work this out in her own mind. Be content to accept her role. Was love enough? That was always the question—the trade off.

A few hours later, she called David from a pay phone. "I just wanted to let you know where I am."

"Let me come get you. Just stay there. I'm coming right now."

By the time he found her, Mariah was wet with sweat. Tear-streaked dirt covered her face. Her hair clung from the humid night. Her white T-shirt was filthy with garage dirt. She was chilled from sobbing. David had never thought she'd gone so far; how far could anyone go on skates?

"Can you take me home? I need to think and I need a break from you to think clearly."

"Let me take you back to the studio to get cleaned up. We need to talk."

"I can't talk to you now," she said, her voice low. "But I will go back to the loft to wash my face and get some stuff." She choked on a sob. "She turned her red eyes to him pleading. "Just take me there. I have to think."

Back home her dad greeted her. "I didn't expect you until midnight at least. Everything all right?"

"I'm fine."

"Have you eaten?"

"You're sweet. Of course. I just needed some space."

Alone in the living room, using the sofa for a bed, Mariah was flooded with memories of the Ranch. Happy thoughts were the best way to cheer up as all her recent plans were tumbling down around her like a falling tower. For the sake of survival, she back peddled fast to Ranch-happy memories.

She remembered her father taking the kids camping all over Texas, from Pedernales State Park to Frederiksberg. She helped arrange the tent in order with knapsacks and sheets and goose down pillows. Their dad had custom designed a box that was large enough to hold everything from camp stove and lanterns to tarps and sleeping bags. Once the box was emptied it doubled as a large picnic table. The whole unit fit on top of the car for easy transport. Their mom used to travel with them, but not these days. This was her chance to grab some peace and quiet. All eight of them were used to camping with their dad. Mariah's was a large Catholic family. She behaved as a good eldest daughter with high responsibility and hard work. Their family obviously didn't believe in birth control or abortion and certainly did not approve of sex before marriage. Abstinence was the sure fire method. Her social life was limited; she stuck close to home, under her parents' watchful eye. Family bonds were strong.

She had been with her Dad for the schoolhouse-building project. Mariah realized she felt as shy and awkward as an adolescent with all these new people, who were well acquainted with one another and with Peter. She switched into quiet observation mode at times like these. She resolved to find a sunny perch and read her great new book on her down time.

That night a feast was planned. The school building had begun with a bang. Lots of bangs and laughter, hammers flew everywhere. The women busied themselves in the makeshift kitchen tent for the well-earned party. Mariah hung around wondering how to help. She didn't really know anyone and no one noticed her hedging along the edge of the group. She soon realized these women had everything under control and didn't need her help. She welcomed the break since at home she was the little mother. She spotted a live oak tree in the late afternoon light and plopped down to read, soon absorbed by the Ayn Rand urban drama. A quiet red haired man strolled up the path. She heard the din of the crowd up at camp and imagined everyone was enjoying cocktails. Solitude was apparently hard to find, even way out here in West Texas.

"Hi," said a soft voice. "May I join you for a moment?"

Mariah glanced up at the tall redhead man as he angled up the hill towards her perch. "Sure," she said, sticking her finger in her book as she closed it.

"I'm Hunter," the quiet intruder introduced himself as he stuck out his hand.

"Hey, I'm Mariah," she said and flashed him a big smile. She took in wise eyes behind wire frame glasses.

"You're Steven French's daughter?"

"My claim to fame, yes." She nodded. "This is our second time here. You look like you know your way around."

"Peter and I are old family friends."

"I love it here, I feel right at home. You know?" She spoke fast when she was nervous.

"You look like you belong here. You look rather...well, like an Indian?" He stared at her thinking she looked more Polynesian than Indian.

"Yes, well I'm not. We're mostly French. It's just the dark hair. And I tan well."

"Polynesian makes sense. More like a Gauguin painting, I'm thinking."

She herself wondered why she looked ethnic, when she was just an ordinary American. "Certainly you look like an English explorer with your fair skin and gentile manners." He wore pants and long sleeves even in this heat.

"Thanks. Mind if I sit?" He sat down cross-legged sharing her tree.

"Be my guest." She smiled, trying to be hospitable, "Are you in college? Well, you are obviously, but what are you studying?"

"Law. I have one year left at the University of Texas."

"Really? That's great! I'm still in high school, but I'd like to go to UT when I graduate."

"What do you plan to study?"

"Architecture."

"What are you reading?" He bent his head to read the title.

"Ayn Rand, Atlas Shrugged. I've already read The Fountainhead, if that's what you're thinking." She abandoned her finger hold in the book. "How do you know Peter?"

"We've been friends for years. We grew up together in San Antonio," Hunter said.

"Well, I like him—what I have seen so far. I'm here with my dad and Matt and Fanny Weston."

"Oh, Matt. He's the architect who is organizing everything for the school."

"Why does Peter want to restore the schoolhouse?" Mariah asked.

"He's an historian. It's his hobby, and it's his way of preserving his inheritance." He studied her face, "This place." He gestured around at the endless horizon that surrounded them.

"It's a big place." Mariah let that fact sink in, 'for one person to own,' she thought. "Hmm. I thought Peter's reasons were more profound than just an accurate historical renovation."

"Would you care to join me?" He extended a hand to help her up. "We can discuss it over dinner."

The two were soon engrossed in conversation at one of the card tables as they ate. He stared at her thinking she definitely looked Polynesian. He made a few more references to Gauguin's paintings. She studied him with a sideways glance, wondering if this was a new sort of compliment. He, like the true fair-haired descendant of explorers who were strangely drawn to all things foreign, dark and mysterious, found himself unexplainably drawn to her. He had spotted her earlier while she was sunbathing in a tropical bikini, her brown body and jet-black hair fit naturally into the landscape of rock and water.

As Mariah listened to Hunter speak, it was as if they were two introverts who found each other. She found him fascinating to converse with. Although he was an advanced law student he was fun, not a snob. She hung out with many of her dad's artist friends. He was probably not your normal lawyer. He was a committed outdoors man. *Here in Texas everyone seemed to have a love for the land.*

Now, on her father's sofa, filled with the scent of his cherry tobacco, she thought of Hunter. What was he up to these days? Now she was fully awake. Her musing brought Mariah to thoughts of Peter St. George. What made him tick?

After dinner, everyone had grouped around the large fire. Mariah glanced up and smiled as Peter strolled up. With his hands in his pockets, he looked more like a guest than a host. Her green eyes danced in the firelight. He smiled.

Hunter found an open bottle of Zinfandel on the table and brought it over with a proper plastic wine glass. Peter poured a glass for her.

"Thanks." They all toasted with an assortment of bottles and plastic cups.

"To summer."

"To new friends."

Peter stood silent, as he held his longneck loosely in slender fingers. Mariah wondered what to say to this unassuming, generous person. She found she liked his soft manner. He slipped in like a ghost, with hardly a ruffle in the airwaves. "I enjoyed our trip backpacking at the Davis Mountains," Mariah said.

"Completely virgin territory. We never saw a soul for three days and nights of hiking out there. Large tracts of America are still untouched wilderness."

"I've heard there is still homesteading in Montana." Mariah looked hopeful.

Peter smiled.

"So we are speculating about your new old schoolhouse. What's the deal?" Mariah asked.

"I thought we could use it as a place for meetings or to teach those who still live out here."

"But I thought when your grandfather bought all the land, the goat farmers and farmers who were eking out a living left and moved to town?"

"That's true partially. The only people who live out here are those who know how to. Yes, I suppose that's true."

The three stared at the fire while the sound of serious voices, mingled with laughter, floated around them. Steven French was in especially good humor. He was smoking his pipe and smiling. Mariah didn't see her sisters anywhere.

Mariah remembered staying huddled in the blanket draped over her shoulders, as she watched castles in the flames of the huge bonfire for hours, before she went back to check on the sleeping children.

With that Mariah slept at last.

CHAPTER 6 *Peter St. Georges*

Peter St. George stuffed his hands deep in his pockets and stabbed the hard earth with the toe of his shoe. Hot dust rose like smoke in the still air. The grass made a hum as it cooked in the heat of the day. He glanced up at the deep cobalt sky. That was it. He was going to stay out here this summer, no matter what. He could still hear his parents' car as it rolled slowly over rocks and through the water of the stream below the house.

That was years ago. As he remembered it, his parents and sisters went off for a two-week trip down to Acapulco to play in the sun. They wanted him to come. This would be their last family trip. They were all too old and too busy to take trips together. Acapulco? Somehow nothing called to him there. His mom wanted to spend time with him, but she just smiled when he said he wasn't going. Let him be, she told his father. He remembered that decision as though it was yesterday. He had been nineteen then.

For Peter, there was endless wealth here at The Ranch. He felt a peace and a strange sense of belonging, more than he had ever felt in San Antonio with his family. That summer he was building a topographical map of the entire territory and he planned to hike the perimeter of the land with a backpack. It would take days. He didn't know what he would find, but he needed to be prepared. He squinted up at the sky. A hawk flew high. Actually this was going to be a nice two weeks. He knew his parents probably told the neighbors to come check on him periodically, but he would be okay.

Peter checked his list of supplies one more time. The youngest in his family, he was used to being alone. He regretted his pale freckled skin that came from his German-Irish heritage. This meant wide-brimmed hats, long-sleeved shirts and lots of sunscreen. Water. Would he have enough water? He loaded a couple of gallons. The springs that fed the rivers were located three miles from the house. He wasn't sure what the perimeter would have.

Five days later he returned. He had made only a small dent in the property. It was tough going. Mostly overgrown brush hills and creek draws. Only parts of the land were fenced, but these were all but destroyed, in some areas completely trampled. It was old barbed wire fencing strung between split cedar logs. On his way back in he had come up through the creek draw that led to Blue Spring. The clear, cold water welcomed him as he looked down at it from the cliff. He ripped his boots and clothes off and shouted, "Woo hoo!" As he dove deep into the seemingly bottomless spring, his hot aching body numbed immediately by the ice water. As he lay on his back staring up at the sky he wished he had someone to share all this with.

After drying off on the rocks, he gathered his clothes and pack, dressed, and trudged happily on. Something strange had happened on that hike. He couldn't quite place it. He had gone days without seeing anyone, yet he felt a presence out there. He heard noises, tons of them. It was damn loud to be honest. But somehow it seemed there were other noises under the loudness of crickets, pounding water, and animal calls. A shot suddenly sounded. The bang of the cattle guard gate, he realized later, but it startled him and he jumped. Company, he thought.

This first test of his independence set the stage for what was going to become his life. He went to college and he participated in the family business, but years later he found himself out here all alone. Comfortable and ensconced in the rhythm of the Texas hill country.

Ten years had flown by and Peter still stood, feet on the ground, hands in his pockets on his bit of Texas he called The Ranch. He glanced up as he heard the splash of a car fording the stream below. Company. He squinted as the smoke cleared.

It must be one o'clock, Peter thought. Hunter had arrived on time. His friend was just as fair and freckled as Peter, with baby fine strawberry blond hair from his Irish ancestry. He wore a cool, long-sleeved white shirt.

"Hunter, hi," Peter said, as he embraced his friend. "You are just in time for lunch."

"You called and here I am." Hunter was now a lawyer in San Antonio, after a stint clerking in Austin. Peter considered him to be his closest friend.

They sat down on Peter's front porch. They sat in silence. Peter letting Hunter take a minute to acclimate after the long hot drive. He smiled as he observed Hunter's demeanor settle in to match the beauty and the calm of the place. An almost immediate effect, he had noticed, with most visitors.

"You are a true friend," Peter said. "Help yourself to a sandwich. Sorry to burn up your day off, but I only have the weekends here to get everything done."

"I'm glad you called. It's been months since I've been out here. It feels so good. What's up?"

"Did you know the last Indian raid in Texas was right here on this property? 1888. They raided Lakeville, but they were right here. That fascinates me."

Hunter nodded, he had a mouth full of pimento cheese, then changed the subject.

"Do you plan to work in your profession?"

"One day perhaps. You know, there are a lot of negotiations going on in San Antonio. I don't have any interest in them, and I don't have a mind for business, but as her only son I have to protect Mom's interest. Dad worries me sometimes. Helen is married and Ruby is engaged. Dad practically forced Ruby to marry Frank, he's much older. She always called him Mr. Gilbert. I was shocked when they announced the engagement. Maybe she'll change her mind and call it off. Either way, I rarely see either of them anymore."

Peter disappeared into the house, returning a moment later with some sandwiches and placed them on the table along with a couple of cold beers. He offered one to Hunter.

"Let me tell you what's on my mind. I've mulled this over for about a year now. As you know, my great grandfather built the Mill. My grandfather took it over and made it what it is today. He was an ace at business. My mom was his only daughter. He left her everything, almost." He took a swig off his longneck.

Hunter studied Peter's face. He'd barely touched his food.

"He left something to me. Something he wanted to pass directly to me, his only male offspring, luckily for me. I never met the old man, though the stories are rich. He was Mom's father and I'm her son, but we are light years apart. Her grandfather, Fredrick, acquired this land gradually.-Paid ten cents an acre for it. I think, Mom told me, he did it for his wife, my great- grandmother. This land was her world. She was passionate about it."

"That sounds like a steal, even for those days," Hunter said. "Pretty good pimento cheese sandwiches, for a bachelor, by the way."

"Thanks. First, he bought the main section - the one with the springs. But then he kept buying up all the surrounding territory. I'm ashamed at the quantity. Yet I am fascinated by the magnitude. Everything he did, every purchase, was always for a reason. Perhaps he thought of this land as an investment for the future. I'm not sure. I don't have the business acumen or desire to run the mill, but I do want to take care of this land. It's my responsibility."

Hunter nodded. "Yes. I know how you feel."

Peter went in and grabbed two more longnecks from the fridge.

"I'm ready for a swim at the Blue Spring." Peter handed Hunter the beer.

"Great." Hunter wiped his mouth.

"Are you up for a hike? Let's take the Jeep and explore from there."

"You read my mind." Hunter grabbed the plates and put them in the kitchen.

CHAPTER 7 *Michelangelo's*

For the first couple of days, Mariah couldn't even talk about her disastrous love life. She had already blown it with Justin. Now she despaired completely. Her sister Kate, who had inherited the family car, came to the rescue and took her to Biraporetti's for pizza and a glass of wine.

"You need to get out more. You have been holed up in that warehouse, spending all your time with him." Kate twirled her white wine glass in one hand as she drove. She always kept a bottle under the seat.

Once they were seated at a cozy four top, in the middle of the cavernous eatery, Kate said, "Now tell me what happened. Start at the beginning."

Mariah told her the whole story. All the years and years of devoted study and struggle. So few had even graduated and now she was just playing house and painting with a starving *artiste*.

"I want to be with him, but I'd rather be a mistress than a wife. Some men mistake their wife for their Mother, not a role I relish. I do want children. I am just nervous about the bedroom scene that one has to go through to get them."

Kate rolled her eyes, "Some mistress you'd make if you are afraid of sex."

"Shh, You don't have to be so blunt, and loud about it."

Kate twirled her glass and smiled knowingly. "You are so spoiled. Justin was always on the road plus he had an entourage. This is the first time you are in a real-life, day in day out, relationship. It's work."

"I'm not afraid of work. I don't want to lose me in the mix."

With her usual perfect timing, Maxine waved to them from across the crowded room just as the waiter placed a steaming pepperoni pizza on the table.

"Hey Mariah. Hey Kate. Dad said you guys would be here. Looks like enough for three."

"Sure help yourself, Maxi, but no wine. You're all of seventeen now aren't you?"

Mariah nodded to Kate in understanding that this talk was temporarily on hold.

"Sixteen, but I can pass for older. Dad always let me have a beer."

"That's when you're at his house," Mariah said.

"I came to join you guys. Are we celebrating?"

"Well in a way, Kate is cheering me up. Helping me to see both sides clearly."

"If you're discussing relationships, David's the best. Forgive him no matter what. By the way, if you're finished with that little address book of yours, I'd like to borrow it," Maxi said.

"Those guys are all in college and you're not out of high school yet," Mariah said.

"Can't hurt to ask." Maxine shrugged, "actually I already took my G.E.D.." She stuck out her tongue. "I can skip the rest of high school."

"I guess you can little sister." They all laughed and ate pizza. "It's fun to have a girls' night out. Away from the house. Or guys."

"Tell us. What are you going to do?"

"Well, I just don't know tonight. I will think about that tomorrow." Mariah was infinitely cheered.

* * *

Mariah was still consumed with thoughts of The Ranch. David was the first guy she had ever invited there. In her mind had been: David-wedding-Ranch. She needed to rethink this. She deserved a trip to the Ranch, no matter what happened with David. She had good friends there—Hunter and Peter. Being with her sisters tonight, made her remember earlier drinking escapades.

After tucking the little kids into sleeping bags in the green army tent, Mariah joined the group gathered around the campfire.

Peter nudged Mariah. "Did you hear about your sisters?"

"No, did I miss something?" She asked.

"I think Kristen was found with a half empty bottle of tequila. She was a bit sick."

"I can imagine. I am so sorry. She's a bit young." Mariah was embarrassed. How would she ever have a life when she always had to look after ever-adventurous sisters?

Peter smiled. "Oh, it's okay. On a more pleasant note, have you noticed this teepee has been set up all weekend?"

Mariah nodded and looked at him, "Yes?" She felt chill bumps all over and thought again about the disappearing figure on the plateau.

"Every night it remains empty. I think it has your name on it."

"Oh really? Could I? I'd love to sleep in it!"

"Well, its Saturday night and spirits are high..." Peter winked at her. Perhaps he didn't blame her for their behavior after all.

"You mean it?" Mariah already imagined the comforting crackle and smoke of the fires as people sang into the night. "I would love to sleep there!"

Later, Mariah found her little charges and gathered four sleepy tousled heads down next to her. With two on each side, they tucked neatly under her arms. They all joined in on the chorus of 'May a circle be unbroken,' until she realized how tired they were.

She gestured to her father, who was smoking a pipe and nodding his head to the music, to help her bed them down. They had to go down the cliff, across the shallow water and to the to the lower grass plain. She thought she heard noises in the trees. She felt eyes watching her.

An Indian stepped back from the cliff and scaled it in the

46

shadows down to the river. He watched as she stepped over rocks with the two sleepy children. A quiet thunk, as pebbles slipped into the night stream. After tucking the little kids, Liz, Josie, Rob, and Maxine into their sleeping bags, she and her Dad turned back to camp. Mariah grinned to herself as she heard her dad's huffy breath mixed with muttered curses as he made his way in the dark behind her.

"I get to sleep in the tepee tonight," she told him. "I think I'm ready to go to bed." Suddenly her whole body felt exhausted, and her eyes burned. Probably irritated by the fire.

Steven stifled a yawn. " I think we all overdid it last night. I can call it a night."

"So the kids will be alright?"

"I'll be with them," he assured her.

"Okay great, Good night then." She leaned over and hugged her Dad and guided him in the direction of their tent. She watched as he plopped down at the picnic table beside a cedar tree, clearly relieved to enjoy the night air alone.

The Indian smiled softly to himself. Brave maiden.

As she strolled quickly back, through a night lit only by the moon, towards a distant fire, she breathed in the scent of cedar filled air. The cold air on her cheek was invigorating. Ah, the second wind, she thought. She tended to get that at night. She could hear the distant music. George was playing the folk tunes everyone knew. Mariah was relived to see that Kate and Kristen had joined the crowd, looking no worse for wear. Hunter was still there too, his arms slung around a twenty-ish girl with long hair. His girl friend?

'Where have all the flowers gone,' was one of the favorites and she knew them all. Her parents had all the Peter, Paul, and Mary albums, as well as a few Pete Seeger's. Fanny and Matt sounded good as they sang along. Others were way off key. Hearing them was a painful reminder of how good her parents sounded together. Mom was a trained soprano, and Dad had a resonant baritone voice.

His voice was mesmerizing when he told stories. It gave a smooth rhythm to his never-ending tales.

She felt Peter's presence by her side before he spoke.

"Your Dad says you are headed to college in the fall, what do you plan to study?"

"Architecture," she said, turning to him.

Peter raised an eyebrow, surprised. "Really?"

"I've always wanted to design buildings. On the other hand, this place is wonderful because there are so few buildings." She noted Peter's interest and warmed to her subject. "We bring in what we need, and we pack it out, leaving nature pristine, untouched. That is the kind of architect I want to be. To work with the land and with nature, making as little disturbance as possible. I want to create spaces that are part of the landscape, and seem natural. There must be a way. That is what I want to learn while I am at University." She took a breath and went on. "Take for instance the teepee, It's tall, and the air floats up from the flaps at the bottom and out of the top, keeping the interior cool. The opening at the top allows smoke to escape and offers a great view of the stars. It is a great example of natural building."

"That is amazing, Mariah, Most people, especially young people, don't truly appreciate the land the way you do."

"Oh Peter," she said, excitement thrilling her voice, "we have been out here almost five days, and I have to say I hate buildings. I do plan to study architecture, and I have already been accepted into the department at UT, but I love the land. I hate how the landscape becomes destroyed with too many useless buildings." She paused, feeling a bit tipsy about the way she was going on. "You know," she said more quietly, "even in places like Houston, there must be someway to build in harmony with the land. By spending time in Nature, I can learn from nature."

Peter gave her an enthusiastic grin. "If anyone can find a way to do it, my money is on you.""

They might have kept talking on into the night, but instead were soon interrupted by a group of rowdy guests on the hunt for more beer. Peter excused himself to help out.

Mariah turned to her sisters . Upon closer inspection, she realized they were still a bit groggy, and told them it was time for bed. As she hugged them the faint smell of alcohol mixed with puke wafted up from their clothes. She shook Kristen but was too tired to explain that you should not drink tequila by the bottle, especially at her age, and as some ones guest. Sometimes, Mariah felt less like Kristen's sister and more like her mother; boring and always in control. With a sigh, she decided to let them be. The hangover the next morning might be more effective than any lecture.

She nodded a weary good night to the others, then pushed against the night wind as she made the uphill hike to the tepee. Despite her weariness, she took a moment to stare out at the velvet dark of star studded night and embraced the amazing vista. Then she turned and crawled inside.

Mariah unrolled her bedroll on the warm sheepskins laid out to welcome her. She took off her shoes, and then settled in. Her eyes grew heavy as she stared at the night through the open flap at the apex. She studied the night sky, while the distant sound of music carried her off to a dream filled sleep.

While she slept, the Indians wove stories around her head, floating with the smoke that wafted in and entered her dreams. They chanted silently in the woods behind the clearing. The grandmother nodded to her son. "Our white eyes brother has rebuilt the schoolhouse. He has chosen a maiden to sleep in the tepee beside our ancestors burial mound. They shook their heads. We will give her the special gifts: the special fertility and protection from the white man's lust. We will sing our song, music like she has never heard. In the strange white world she lives in, she will need it. She is already a mother to her own mother's children. She has many to care for and believes in the way of the nurturer. Her own children shall be special."

For Mariah, it was like being drugged. She dreamed many dreams –the strangest and most vivid of her life.

In one: *she flew away to another country, crowded and full of apartment buildings. The buildings were modern concrete and steel structures with balconies all the way around. The streets were wall-to-wall asphalt, running from building to building without any space for grass or trees. She flew over as if her body was a bird and then landed on a rusted steel railing. Then she saw hundreds of people. All homeless and wrapped in sleeping bags, fitted neatly on the balcony like sardines. An effective use of space she thought. An engineer must have designed this.*

Then she leapt off the railing and flew, hovering just above the lone leafless treetop. She watched the day just breaking on the sleeping scene. She flew from the crowded chaos and found herself by the sea. When she saw the water, she flew down and plunged in, swimming through the sea as if she were a fish. A light glittered through the water like diamonds. She swam swiftly towards it, then burst forth into the sky and flew like a bird toward the sun.

The next morning Mariah had awoken early. She sat up, with none of her usual morning grogginess. She felt amazing, completely at peace and whole. She needed nothing. The peace was a warmth that spread from the tips of her feet through her chest and pulsated in her fingertips. She stood up and walked over to the flap of the teepee and pulled it open. The sun began its ascent over the valley, casting diamonds on the water of the river below.

She had been sixteen, and from that moment on no one could tempt her with anything. She had known the sublime and she carried that within her. Wherever her life took her, she could close her eyes and be *one* again, on that cliff overlooking the sunrise valley. She stepped lightly upon the earth, knowing she was but a visitor—*on* the earth, yet not *of* the earth.

Just thinking about the Ranch cheered her up. She had her

answer. She could not be consumed by a man, she would always hold her own self-hood. No matter how tempting being consumed by love seemed to be. She resolved to go visit Peter no matter what.

* * *

"That's it!"

Mariah awoke to the smell of coffee brewing, and sat straight up. All week she'd had ranch filled dreams. Hunter and Peter had totally understood her because she'd explained it all clearly over the many years she knew them. Yet, did David have a clear picture? They hadn't been together very long at all. Since she'd met David, she'd quit her Architecture job and gleefully began painting full time in his massive art studio. He probably didn't realize she took architecture so seriously. Face it. She was love crazed. Love made you lose your head. She'd always wanted to have several months to develop her art, to see if there was anything there. After her trip to Paris to study at the atelier, she needed time to practice all the old masters techniques.

The moment she'd returned, she'd begun working full time and painting in the evenings. That left no time for friends, let alone romance. Now that she was hanging with David full time, she'd moved out of her rental house, and moved in with her dad—mostly as a crash pad at night. Once they were married, they would live together full time. Her career was architecture, while David had clients and gallery shows, a full-fledged art career. She cherished this chance to develop her paintings, but that didn't make her less devoted to her architecture career. She needed to be sure they were both clear and honest with one another—on the same page; in alignment—before they made a fatal mistake and got married. She'd been engaged before, and she and Justin couldn't agree on which state to live in. She wanted New York and he'd wanted Nashville.

Funny thing though, she would live anywhere with David. There's that love thing again, she thought. She had it bad. She wanted to marry him and have a fully committed honest and physical relationship. She was not planning to become 'little miss

Housewife,' or 'Home baker.' 'Art wife' she could handle.

She'd been helping to support her family ever since she was sixteen with odd jobs like waitressing. Thank god for scholarships. She had made it through college debt free. These few months in an art studio were a blessing, not a lifestyle.

It was fine she couldn't be in the big 'Fresh Paint' art show. But if she kept working, her time would come one day. She was sure. Almost. Well she was sure she loved David.

* * *

Now, after a week-long separation—when neither of them could no longer stand it —Mariah was ready when David drove up in his well-loved white pickup to take her out to dinner.

"Let's take your backpack and paints just in case you change your mind when you hear me out on this," David begged.

They went to Michelangelo's, an Italian restaurant in Montrose. It was Mariah's favorite, and as it was expensive, they seldom went. Their presence here was evidence of David's determination to win her over.

"How can you afford this?" She breathed, as an army of wait staff pulled out chairs, poured water and placed napkins in their laps, then promptly disappeared while soft jazz piano emanated from the bar.

"They paid an advance on the new sculpture commission."

"Congratulations. Did you get the Allen Parkway project?"

"Sure. What did you expect?" He studied her face, searched her eyes. The strains of *'Love is Blue'* floated from the piano. "Mariah, I'm not sure why you're upset. But I do know we can work it out."

"I think I have commitment issues." She twisted her sweaty hands on her napkin. "I was engaged before, but this is so real...I could see my future flash before my eyes. I want so badly to have a career and after six years of college... It's not your fault. It's love. It gets in the way. I love you. I don't want to lose myself. You can't understand that. It's my own fault."

"You are the first person I have ever let into my space. I love your work, both your art and your architecture. I respect that about you. I will go to New York if that's what you want. You need to know that."

Mariah didn't speak, only studied his storm-teal eyes and the candlelight dancing on his sharp nose and firm serious mouth.

"The bottom line is, I want you. I see my future with you. We belong together. This is the first time we have actually been apart since the New York trip. I want to marry you and grow old together. Please say you'll marry me."

"You mean you do understand about my career?"

"And your art. I love that about you. You paint from your true self. You don't just follow the trends or what's cool." David choked up a bit. "Hey, I just want to be together. Whatever we do. Let's do it together."

Mariah was speechless. "I am not cool or popular. I even like this music."

She listened to the strains of the piano now playing *Beyond the Sea*, and the tinkling of silverware mixed with murmurs of surrounding voices. Life *with* him. Life *without* him. Now that she knew him, there was no longer a real choice for her.

She waited, letting the sound of music fill the air between them. Then watching his serious fragile face, as light and shadow played across his features, she was suddenly all smiles. "Of course I want to marry you."

The melody of Bobby Darren's *Beyond the Sea*, filled the space as David's eyes grew wide, darker, and intense in the candlelight.

"I will marry you," she clarified. "When's the date?"

His electric smile hit her gut. "Now I can enjoy this dinner. Shall we order?"

"Pepperoni Pizza?"

"No way."

CHAPTER 8 *Hill Country Camping*

The arrangements were made. The camping trip to the hill country was eminent. Mariah wasn't sure if all the excitement she felt for her anticipated wedding day wasn't also for this long awaited return to The Ranch.

Intensity magnified the last week before the wedding. They planned the ceremony for nine a.m. After the garden luncheon, wine, and champagne they had ample driving time. It was tight, but they made it out of Houston in front of the traffic.

Hill after hill, they wound their way for endless hours through the state of Texas. Mariah sat cross-legged in the front seat of the Chevy Nova with the "just married" foam still stuck to parts of the back window. She glanced at her husband's handsome profile, then down at the red rose he had pinned to her white T-shirt. The rich velvety petals hung, but the scent was strong. She sighed as she rested her head on his shoulder. Mariah liked roses...and champagne. She twisted the platinum eternity band he had placed on her finger just this morning. They'd had lots of champagne. They were alone finally. After a solid week of family, friends, and people pleasing, they were married. With a Catholic ceremony that went from the church, outside through the stone arbor to the strains of a lone violin, to the Rose Garden where they took their vows in front of God and a deep Texas blue sky.

The road was getting beautiful now, hilly and greener since they passed San Antonio. Must be a lot of rain out here, David thought.

He felt exhausted in a peaceful kind of way, having been up late with pre-marital nerves. At least the Nova was running okay. He just hoped he could get the rest of that just-married stuff off of the car. All this show was embarrassing.

"He has satin pillows," Mariah said, "out here in the middle of nowhere. The cabin has a big dorm area with a lot of beds in it and a huge hammock on the porch. The three of us sisters would just lie in the hammock watching the stars, and drinking Kahlua. And laugh. We could laugh for hours. Guys don't understand that sort of thing." She felt just like a girl as she recalled this. She should grow up and be serious now. "There are more stars out there than anywhere in the world."

"Look, Mariah, I'm sure it's a great place. I'm glad we're going, but you have to know, I'd go anywhere with you." He grinned.

Mariah stuck her tongue out at him. "I've traveled all over, you know, I'm not making this up. The Ranch is great. I speak from experience."

David smiled. It was fine with him. It was all fine. "Do you think you will recognize the turn- off when we get there?"

"Sure," she replied, her brow furrowed. What if she couldn't find it? That would be bad. "It's been ages since I've been there. This is the place I longed for when I lived in New York City. I wrote poetry about it—standing on New York rooftops, looking at the city like a big canyon of stone, all the while longing for a different canyon of rock—Texas rock. Once a Texan, always a Texan. I love Texas." She made a sweeping motion with her hand. "This is the Texas I love."

By five o'clock they had arrived at the fourth river crossing. They could see the stone house perched just behind the cedar trees.

Peter came out to greet them. Mariah jumped out of the car as soon as it stopped and ran to give him a big hug.

"You can't be Mariah! You're so grown up!"

She waved away what she took as a compliment. "How are you doing?"

"Great. Fine. I'm out here full time now." Peter squinted up at the sky, then adjusted his ball cap and put his hands back in his pockets.

"This is my husband, David," she said, enjoying the feel of the unfamiliar phrase on her tongue.

Peter held out a hand to David. "Good to meet you. Do you need some help with your stuff?"

"No, we're fine, I'll grab it in a minute."

"Peter, is it too late for a swim? I thought we could show David the swimming hole at Big Rock this evening."

"Of course, have at it. Warning you, though, the water's cold."

"Thanks." Mariah gave him a quick peck on his cheek. "Which room is ours?"

"Follow me." Peter led the way through the kitchen and toward the bedrooms. "Hunter and his wife will be up here tomorrow."

"He's married? I can't believe it. I guess I haven't stayed in touch very well. Are you going to join us for a swim, Peter?"

"I'll walk down there with you."

"It smells great here, all that cedar," David said, and was rewarded with a brilliant smile from Mariah.

"It's great, right? I told you." Mariah hopped beside him in excitement.

"The creeks are high," Peter interjected. "We've had a lot of rain this spring. You can use the blue and white jeep to explore the area while you're here."

"Thanks. It's a great place you have." David had to admit he was a bit awestruck, especially later, when Mariah scrambled up Big Rock and dove into the deepest part of the creek. "It's cold," she screamed.

Peter laughed.

"Aren't you swimming? She asked. She had to swim fast to keep warm. It was a creek, not a river, but it was wide and cut through the tall marshy grasses. It was crystalline water. Golden pebbles shone below her feet. Big boulders shone white against the deep green blue where the water ran deepest.

David kicked off his shoes and waded in, his feet going numb in the icy water. "I can see why you call it Big Rock," he said, staring at the huge white limestone boulder.

"Are you coming in?"

"You go ahead. We have all week to swim."

"Hey, go on in," Peter nodded. "It will totally refresh you after that drive."

Mariah floated on her back. Gliding, on the glass flat water, she watched a hawk spiral up in the blue sky high above their heads. She watched the bird for a long time, all else forgotten as the water beneath her fell away and left her floating in total equilibrium. She realized with the air clean and clear, the sky was a long way up. The hawk floated in circles higher and higher, shrinking to miniature. Seeing her peaceful meditation, David grabbed Peter's arm to talk about fishing and headed back up to the house.

The sun glowed a deep orange beyond the tall spears of grass, which tossed in the quick evening breeze. Mariah strolled back to the house towards the flames in the distance. She was still chilled as she joined the men, grateful for the warmth of the small fire.

"Have some wine?" David handed her a glass of red Zinfandel. "Cheers." They toasted the day, the sunset, and one another. Mariah excused herself to change. Peter filled David in as he prepared to grill some steaks and start the potatoes. Mariah came back wearing a long colorful gypsy patterned skirt wrapped tight around her waist. Her still wet dark hair was combed straight back. She carried a wooden bowl filled with a green salad.

"This is a big place," Peter was saying. "There are some sites to see. I'll give you a tour. Show you how to find the main attractions. Then you can use the Jeep and three-wheelers to get around on your own."

The next morning they decided that sleeping in the cabin with satin pillowcases was definitely the way to go. They could still cook at their campsite and keep all the comforts of a real bed at night. After all, things in the bedroom were hard enough without throwing hard ground and rocks into the mix. When sleeping alone has been a way of life, sleeping together added a whole new dimension to it. This was the first night they would spend together as a couple. Mariah thought about the middle ages, when newlyweds had an audience just beyond the bedchamber to assure consummation of the union.

Mariah was shivering from a combination of icy water, exhaustion...and fear. This was the hard part about being married, she'd decided. David had spent the night before caressing every inch of her body. She was tingling all over as he began kissing first her fingertips, then he moved on to the tender side of her soft flesh, like the inside of her arms, and then her thighs. The dance between the sheets soon had pillows and blankets falling to the floor. Then, as she shivered with the excitement of new sensations, he warmed her with a sensuous embrace that soon had both of their bodies entwined like the Rodin marble sculpture, 'The Lovers'. After the initial exhilaration, she may have fallen asleep in shear exhaustion, only to be awakened with kisses in the still dark morning.

As she prepared breakfast the next morning, the mere thought of the awkward encounter tangled her emotions and she blushed crimson. Mariah tried instead to focus on the task at hand—her attempt at an omelet for David's breakfast. She hurriedly scraped scrambled eggs out of the iron skillet before they burned.

"I hope it's edible," she grinned sheepishly as she slid the pile onto a plate. "I don't want to be discarded before the honeymoon is over." She resolved to master the art. David was a great teacher.

Using a fork, David somehow managed to toast the tortillas over the little campfire stove flame. They ravenously devoured the meal. Appetites were sharpened in the cool morning air. It's amazing what a little hot sauce forgives, she thought.

After breakfast Peter greeted Mariah with a cheery hello. He was in the courtyard with a huge telescope. All three took turns watching the Moon eclipse the Sun. He had set the scope beneath a sycamore tree with a view of the sky. Peter pointed to the ground.

There Mariah could see the pattern of the leaves shadow mirrored the passage in the sky. Tiny eclipses were all over the ground, multiplied like a prism. Mariah was amazed their honeymoon was, quite by accident, during a solar eclipse. There was something eternal about contemplating the movement of sun and moon. She studied her simple wedding band again, with its tiny diamonds a continuous circle set in platinum. She liked commitment after all.

When they finished, they loaded up the jeep with a cooler and supplies for their trip to Indian Point. The day had an auspicious air to it. David and Mariah were silent as they drove. David broke the silence.

"What kind of Indians used to live here?"

Mariah shrugged. "The Apaches, I think, but I don't know a lot about Texas Indians. I do know, Indian Point is a burial mound."

CHAPTER 9 *Adam and Eve*

After a day of swimming, Mariah's muscles burned with a pleasant tinge. It was dusk before they arrived at base camp, she, still dizzy headed, partly from nerves, as evening drew near. Together they arranged the logs, big ones for the main fire and a smaller stone circle to cook on.

"I think I'm hungry, I know we had a late breakfast, but now…"

"You're not sure if you're hungry?" David approached behind her and encircled her in a hug. He looked out over her head at the cliffs glowing amber in the sunset. The sound of river over rocks in the background, chattered like a constant companion. She looked at him sideways over her shoulder and tried to reach his lips. Smiling, he gently rotated her until their faces met, and then the newlyweds kissed, a chaste meeting of lips, before melting into an embrace. The warmth of his arms around her reminded Mariah how safe she felt with him, especially here. As she hugged him her eyes glanced at the Mound. They were standing at sunset on nineteen thousand acres of land and only seven people at most were scattered about in their separate reveries.

"I'll go fetch some salad," she said, pulling gently away. Salad was a pile of lettuce and spinach in a bowl with olive oil and vinegar sprinkled on it. Nothing fancy.

When she returned, they grilled two thick steaks on the flame. David had the potatoes wrapped in foil and baking in the coals. They watched the fire, and the stars in the sky come out, one by one.

"I don't know why we always end up eating in the dark," Mariah said.

"I do. You always want one more swim or hike to the cliff paintings. I'm just glad we got back here before sundown. At least we could cook before dark."

She smiled and toasted him with her jelly glass of Malbec. "It's just that I want to hold onto each minute of daylight. I watch the sun and I want it to hold still. I want each day to last forever. I want this week to last forever."

"The nights too?" David smiled.

"Yes," Mariah said.

"We are in the Garden of Eden you know. You should be careful what you wish for."

"Garden of Eden?" Mariah raised her eyebrows at him.

"Well, look around you. The fish for one. You can see whole schools through the water. There are tons of plants, roots, and berries. I'm sure Indians would know how to gather them and live off the land. There are deer, wild turkey, rabbits, goats, and who knows what else lives here in these woods."

"It's true. The water is so pristine you can drink from the springs. There are caves for shelter. That's what I mean. I wish each day could last. When I look up at the sun it seems I can see it visibly moving in the sky. Suddenly it's gone and here we are once again, eating our delicious gourmet meal on a blanket, our plates in our laps, in front of the fire in the dark."

He squeezed her hand, a thank you for bringing him to this place. "I love every minute of it. Remind me, what kind of Indians lived here?"

She shrugged. "Not sure. Hey, you know I slept here in a teepee by myself when I was sixteen."

"Seriously?"

"Yeah. Actually, it was Peter's idea. The next morning I came out of the tent in my white cotton nightgown and watched the sun rise over the point. I could see all the other campers, down in the meadow by the river. Outwardly everything looked as it had the day before, yet something had shifted. I felt different; it was as though

I was an Indian girl in a simple white deerskin dress. My skin was so dark back then I probably looked the part. I have always felt I belonged here after that. But it never even dawned on me that an Indian mound was a grave. Are we sitting now with the ancestors of this land? The real owners?"

Before he could reply, she answered the question. "No, they never felt that they were owners either. It's impossible to own land. We can use it, borrow it, plant it, and harvest it, but not own it. It's like the Great Mother. It would be like owning a person. The land just is."

They both jumped as a bloodcurdling scream tore the fabric of darkness.

"A wildcat?" Mariah asked, leaning against him. "This close to us?" She stared at the velvet darkness that surrounded them. She realized she couldn't see a thing beyond the comforting circle of fire.

"By the water, probably. Animals need water too."

"I'm scared."

"Don't be. It's just nature."

She gave him a sideways glance. David always took things in stride.

"I wish they never lost the Garden of Eden."

"What?"

"Adam and Eve."

"I like this game," he said softly. "You can take all your clothes off if that's the case."

"Tomorrow," she said.

"Tell me more about the tepee."

"Well, Peter had invited all his friends out to build this little red schoolhouse. Matt was the supervising architect and my dad was the photographer. Peter invited our whole family; for some reason he was fascinated that there were seven sisters and two brothers. There were food tents, picnic tables, and outdoor toilets set up. Sleeping areas were by the river." Her voice was wistful with the remembering. "It was wonderful for me. Old enough to spend time off by myself, but young enough to not have a lot of responsibility.

And no one seemed to want me or my sisters to help build the schoolhouse. Kristen, Kate and I spent whole days at Jade Cove, just sunbathing, watching dragonflies, and snorkeling for hours at a time. I was drawing a lot back then, so I brought my sketchbook…"

"I think they are Apache," David said.

"Hum?"

"The Indians from around here…they're Apache."

"They were the savage, violent ones, weren't they?"

"Mariah, how can you say that? Do you believe everything Hollywood puts on the screen? The popular culture is created by myths invented by the media."

She shrugged. No arguing with that. "How can we know the truth?"

"By being out here. Living it. This is their world. You feel their spirit permeate the place, and when we're here, we somehow join in that spirit."

"Yes. I can feel it," she said, inhaling as if to take it all in. "When there are tons of people around it's easy to forget how virgin this land is. Like the night I went into the teepee, it was loud while I was falling asleep, people smoking marijuana and playing guitars by the fire. I just drifted off to the sounds of music…" Her voice trailed off and it was like she had travelled back there for a moment. "But when it's this dark and quiet, and just the two of us, I can really feel them—the Indians. I feel their presence all around. This is a sacred spot."

"They lived out here for centuries." David grew quiet.

A wind blew up from the water. David tightened his grip around Mariah's shoulders. She looked into his eyes for a second, then by some silent, unspoken agreement, they reluctantly stood and began loading the jeep. It was time to go back to the cabin.

* * *

"Where did you find this arrowhead?" Mariah was fingering a particularly large one from a box Peter had in the dining room.

"Out in the dust," Peter shrugged. "They turn up from time to time."

Mariah placed the box on the table and continued poking through it. Peter had quite a collection. "Were there several tribes living out here, or were they all Apache?"

"This was Apache territory, for the most part." He always had been one for short answers; it made her feel like she was prying.

She waited a moment, then asked, "Do you ever get lonely out here?"

"Well, I go to San Antonio on family business at least once a month—I'm on the board of the company. Other than that I'm here, seven days a week, but not always alone. I have company most weekends during the summers." He shrugged again. "I like it both ways—the quiet weeks, and busy weekends. There is a lot of work out here, you know." He winked. "San Antonio's fine, but I definitely prefer it out here."

"I guess." She smiled to cover up her disbelief of anyone content to be completely isolated and alone.

She could keep some thoughts to herself.

CHAPTER 10 *Genius*

Time passed. David and Mariah, bounded by something deep and eternal, remained newlyweds much longer than most couples, even after the kids came along. By year seven, they were ensconced in a wonderful, rambling, old house, with a mortgage they thought was a small price to pay for all the happiness it afforded them. Their two precious children—a son, Tristan and a daughter, Isabella—kept life interesting. As well as an assortment of jobs that artists tend to string together to make it all work. Everything about their life was stimulating, and even within the mundane world of the suburban family, little was predictable.

"The thing about having geniuses for kids," complained Mariah as she plopped down on the couch, eliciting a cry from a squeaky toy, "is they learn to talk too soon. They get into important schools and have too much homework, too soon, and the worst is, they think they are smarter than I am."

It was nine p.m., nearly the end of a very long day.

"I know, and you went to Rice," David mocked her.

"That's right, I must be smart." Mariah grimaced as she got up again and went into the kitchen. There were still dishes to be washed.

"Sounds like you and I need a trip to The Ranch," David said as he followed.

"The Ranch," she sighed. Just the thought of the place was like a soothing balm. Her heart rate went down several degrees.

"It's hot as hell in Houston. The kids can't stay outside all day, and I know Tristan beats you at chess."

She pulled her hands from the sink and flicked water at him. "I feel like an old hag – always with a dish rag on my shoulder and a hankie in my hair. But they are cute when they're asleep."

"That's a do-rag. It's cool." David tagged her with a clean dish towel lying on the counter.

"You know, you have a point," she said, as she dodged the towel. "The kids have never been to The Ranch. Just think how fun it will be for them. But Isabella's only three. Do you think she will be able to hack it? Climb the cliffs and swim in that ice-cold water?"

"You already taught her how to swim and she's strong." David cornered her.

Mariah snuck out from under his arm, then stopped mid-escape and turned. "Ice-cold water. The thought of it cools me off."

"One day we will be able to afford air-conditioning. I'm working on paintings for a new show." He pinned her back against the fridge.

"That's good. We'll be fine one day, but now it's all vegetables, sweat, and hard work." She grimaced at the sight and smells of him, though she secretly liked it.

David poured a glass of white wine and handed it to her. "Keep thinking: ice cold water, cedar campfires, grilling steaks on the fire in the evenings, and whole days full of sunbathing and swimming. We can float down the river in the glass-bottom boat."

She took it gratefully. "Well, for an artist you are pretty brilliant."

He toasted her glass. "I *am* brilliant. I just keep it hidden under my cool exterior."

Mariah smiled for the first time all day. Just the thought of The Ranch took creases from her forehead.

She tiptoed to the bedroom door to check on her two kids. Isabella looked so sweet and clean, curled up in the twin bed asleep. It was the matching twin bed set from David's childhood. Isabella was a big help already as an independent Montessori kid. She was advanced for three, as she trailed her six-year-old brother, Tristan, and his friends around. She loved bugs, so she helped her Dad in the vegetable garden, picking all of the snails from under the leaves of the spinach, lettuce and kale plants. She never met a puddle she didn't jump in with both Stride-rights on her feet.

Tristan was precocious. He was already writing elaborate stories about lost treasure in his Montessori classroom. He had a big imagination. They used creative spelling, so a kid could write what ever they wanted, and sound out the words they couldn't spell properly. These words would become their spelling list. Now his language skills were catching up to his vocabulary. Each child could advance at his own rate. The teacher read his stories out loud to the younger kids.

Tristan had a lot of energy. To focus it, Mariah had tried the Houston Ballet when he was five, pulling strings to get him a part in The Nutcracker. David put his foot down on that one. His boy in tights was not an image he could live with. Mariah had to concede because Tristan had fallen down three times during the audition. Tristan insisted they were Pratt falls. He was just trying to lighten up the crowd of terrified kids. Mariah loved dance. Ah well.

She had fond thoughts of them while they were sleeping. They would adore the Ranch. Why hadn't she thought of it before?

Mariah herself had once wanted to be a dancer. Yet her life had taken a more serious turn out of necessity. Both her parents were dreamers; someone had to be smart about finances. Her dad studied theology in the seminary, and became a professional photographer. Her mom studied Philosophy and had a master's degree in English. Nine kids had survived in tact. Most of them had creative careers. Philosophy gives one a good backbone for life skills. Her Mom loved to quote Kahlil Gibran, from his book "The Prophet." She often repeated the part about children. 'And though they are with you, they belong not to you…You are the bows from which your children, as living arrows, are sent forth.' So Mariah had lived her life between the philosophical insights of her Mother's wisdom, The Prophet, and the Book of Wisdom, in the Bible. Along with the cliché saying, 'God helps those who help themselves,' she never sat still waiting. She took action and solved problems. When she was a teen, that meant, work hard and put yourself through college, if you want a degree. She glanced up at David, who'd joined her at the door.

"Come here. Sit on my lap." He took her by the hand and led her back to the living room couch.

She took in his paint-splattered clothes, messy hair, unshaven jaw and blue eyes. Then she climbed on top of him. The best part was, he was all hers, every paint chip in his thick wavy hair. Whether they were painting paintings, or painting houses, they would survive.

CHAPTER 11 *Geronimo's Story*

At long last, the Agnelli's were almost there. Speeding down the two-lane HI way past all the small towns, David veered the Suburban onto HI way 50, the last leg of the journey. For Mariah, it always felt like the six-hour drive out of a chaotic, contemporary, civilization, and back into a time out of time.

"Oh no, here we go again," Mariah said.

"What?" David asked.

"I don't think I can remember the turn off. It all looks so similar," Mariah said.

"Who's your daddy? I've got this," David said.

The tape in the car was singing 'throw it out the window, the window, the window,' for the 13th time. Isabella still giggled every single time. Then the car lurched as David took a sharp turn off the main rode and onto a rutted one, and is if by magic, the song ended and everyone in the car seemed to hold their breaths.

They went about 100 yards through the brush before they came to a red cattle gate. A yellow sign read 'Keep Out.' They slowed for a moment, then David pushed on through and the gate swung open. The road was a tunnel of live oaks. An intimidating tangle of deep brush lined both sides. The kids rolled down their windows and hung out, one on each side, seat belts forgotten. The bird sounds were loud. Frightened deer scampered out of the way as the huge Suburban crashed through. The dark tunnel of trees went on for miles before they came to the first river crossing.

"OK kids, we are officially on Ranch land now. We must cross four rivers before we get to Peter's house," Mariah said. "Number

We are not alone. We are all in this together.

one."

"Number one," they all shouted.

The tunnel opened up to a wide prairie. And they crossed the second stream.

"Piece of cake," Mariah said.

"Are you nervous?" David asked.

"Yes. You know my dad and all of us got stuck the very first time we came out here."

"Ah yes, I well remember the story."

"River number two," everyone shouted in unison.

Now the gravel road widened and the road went through a rushing stream. Water glinted silver, with the bank a bit higher on the other side.

"Can we make it guys?" David asked.

"Yes! Go for it. Yay."

Now Mariah could see the familiar sight of the stone house, just beyond the silver maple leaves. Mariah squeezed David's hand.

"We're here. It's been seven years."

"That's true, I had lost count."

"Isabella is three, and Tristan is six, and seven years ago was our honeymoon and a solar eclipse."

Soon, after greeting Peter, and reminiscing over lost years, David and Mariah set up camp on Indian Point.

"Mom, Mom, tell us a story," Tristan and Isabella chimed together.

"Yes please, a story," Isabella said.

It was almost dark and they sat around a blazing cedar campfire. The castles in the flames always entranced her. Despite the heat of the day, the fire was welcome. She was glad to carry on the tradition her dad had begun. Mariah pulled her memory back to her dad's old stories about The Ranch.

She was lost in thoughts about the Teepee. She had never asked

Peter how he had come to have it. Tristan and Isabella never tired of the tale although they had heard about the magic teepee before. Smiling, Mariah remembered that night so long ago.

"Where do you get your stories, Mom?" Isabella asked.

Mariah tuned back in to her daughter wondering how to frame that into a tale she could tell. Not tonight, she decided.

"I get them from the wind. Especially here. They just float into my head. From the rocks too, the rocks have stories to tell. You know, we would always gather around the big campfire to hear your Grandfather tell stories."

She had listened to her father's stories at the fireside since she was little. He always began, "*Once upon a time there were three sisters...*" That was them, of course, Kate, Kristen, and Mariah. The stories were always epic adventures, deep into mysterious caves and forgotten deserts. She knew that he would end with "*to be continued...*" It was appropriate. Now her dad had friends whose lives seemed to flow from one party to the next. After a while her childhood of never ending stories had become one endless string of parties and camping trips.

"*You know this is Indian Territory?*" Mariah began. Her dad had addressed her in that way when he began a tale. She always went along with it. And so she began the tale for her own kids as she simultaneously recalled the past.

"*Well, Dad, are you going to tell us a story about Indians? A mystery perhaps?*" she would ask. She remembered her father quietly puffed his pipe, amidst the popping and the spitting, and the lick of orange flames. He paused to let out his long familiar sigh. That's when he knew he had them; seven sisters and the little brother who would soon nestle to sleep in one of their laps.

"*Tonight's story is about a hero—the greatest Indian hero, in my book.*" She heard his voice in her head as she recounted the tale for her kids. "*And yes, it's a mystery, in a way.*"

All eyes had been on him as he gathered his tobacco and filled his pipe, packing it smooth with his thumb. The younger ones jostled for their places in the laps of Kristen, Kate and Mariah.

"What's this guy's name?" Kristen asked.

"*The great Indian hero, Geronimo.*" He rubbed his hands together in anticipation.

Kristen rolled her eyes. "Everyone knows about Geronimo."

"Ah, but the secrets I am about to reveal are known only by a very few." He puffed his pipe. "*Geronimo was an American Indian who belonged to the tribe called Apache.*"

"Aren't those the bad Indians?" Kate squirmed as she spoke, "The warrior types that fight all of the other peaceful Indians?"

Steven waved her away. "Hollywood. You girls need to listen to my stories and not believe everything you see on television. Now, where was I? *Ah yes, Geronimo was an Apache Indian Chief.*" He resumed his story in a smooth melodious baritone.

"*The tribe had a huge territory that extended from New Mexico out to the Hill Country in Texas to the east and Chihuahua, Mexico to the west. The large area encompassed a lot of desert, mountains, rivers and forests, in all, a very diverse and hostile terrain.*" Their dad paused for another puff of his pipe.

"Are we sitting on Indian land now?" Rob wanted to know.

Maxine just wanted him to get on with it. "Yes, silly. This whole country is Indian land."

"I meant," Rob repeated his question, "Is *this* land Apache land?"

"Yes, I am glad you asked that. Rightfully, it is. Peter says his grandfather practically stole the land; he paid so little for it. Peter does his part to keep it in its original condition. It's called land stewardship." He looked expectantly at their faces to make sure they understood. At their nods, he continued.

"*Geronimo was a brave warrior and a medicine man to his people. He was magnificent of stature, with sleek brown muscles and long black hair. The Apache has few possessions. He has himself, with his natural gifts of strength and courage, and being a warrior culture, a good dose of cunning. But even more important than his cunning was his wisdom. He has his wife, children, and family. But most precious of all, key to the survival of his tribe, he has his land."*

All were silent now.

"His land is big and vast and he honors the land of his birth, by traveling upon it, living with it, from it, and on it. Through the thousands of years of living, the Apache knew exactly how to move with the land for the plants and game in season. Everything they knew they learned from a story, and everything they knew they passed on with a story. They had no written language. The Indian lived on his land with his story. His story was his land, and his land was his survival.

"His life was very different from the white man's, who was stuck in one place where he built a dwelling for himself and filled it with all he owned. He owned his stuff, his wife, his kids, his patch of dirt, his guns, even his animals. Everything was fenced in and possessed. All the Apache had was grand. He had the vast sky above and her ornament, the rainbow. The wind beat across the desert, the hawk circled above in the sky. He was in nature and of nature. From it he gained his sustenance and life. He honored the land and the earth by walking upon and listening to her. In this way, Geronimo grew up and he was no different than any Apache before him. And I would like to say, none after. But that is no longer true. Although the heart of Geronimo was right and good and true, he was born into a world that was changing." Steven paused to smile at the lovely faces of his children lit by the fire.

As she had listened, Mariah glanced away from the light into the velvet black sky. Her attention drifting, she remembered when her dad took the family to visit the Pueblo Indians in New Mexico when she was only five. She had met the Chief. He was clearly chiefly. She remembered he wore a huge feather headdress. He was dressed in full regalia, leather and lots of long fringe on his sleeves. He had wanted especially to meet *her*. He gave her a beaded necklace as a gift. Her dad had offered to pay, but the Chief waved him off. It was a gift. There she was, a little white girl in her red dress, staring up into the face of that dark-skinned Indian. The pungent cedar aroma brought her back to the sound of her dad's voice.

"*The boundary of Geronimo's land was a story. During his day, it extended from the edge of the plain where the bluebonnets grew in spring, all the way to the stone cliffs. But then, all of a sudden people were showing up on all sides who didn't know the story. They were operating from a different script, coming from another world view; they had made carefully drawn maps with lines and boundaries. Thus, they labeled the frontier. In one part of the Apache's land were the Mexicans and Spanish. In another part, a log cabin with a family called settlers, could be found. The Apache were devastated. They could not comprehend the changes.*

"It would be like coming down from the third floor bedroom of your mansion and going to eat in the far end dining hall, only to find a whole family of strangers eating there, as if they owned the place. Indignantly, instead of asking permission or apologizing, they complain of your appearance in your nightgown at their diner.

"*Geronimo grew up in a world gone topsy-turvy. What had been instilled in him was a way of life that fed his very soul. As the earth and the land nurtured him, the Indian gave back by living with it and giving thanks to the Great Spirit. These concepts are like the wind, unseen and powerful at the same time. The sunsets are the paintings in the sky that adorn their world. Taking and giving back was as natural as breathing to them. You know, as you take in new air, you exhale old air.*

"*Geronimo was born into this time of change. And as both Shaman to his people and a fierce warrior, he had to come to terms with the changes in their world.*"

"*He had to decide what to do about the battles, fights, and raids on their territory, their home. When their village was plundered and women and children were brutally murdered, Geronimo lost his wife and two sons.*

"*Confusion and rage stormed his soul. He tore his clothes and covered himself in dirt and ashes. He ran for days. He was confused.*

He had been betrayed by the Great Spirit of the universe. The US government offered them peace in exchange for their land. The pitiful offer of a small corner of New Mexico where the Apache could build houses and grow crops.

"Well to Geronimo, this was a death sentence—death to the Apache way. He reasoned that the death of the Apache would follow. With all his body, strength, and spirit, Geronimo fought the US government.

Finally, the Indian Elders and his own people agreed to the treaty. Thousands of Apache were herded to one small corner of New Mexico. It was a beautiful spot near the mountains, called Ruidoso today. Geronimo still resisted. He could not forget the crimes against his family. He took his son, Naiche, and a small band of followers, braves, women, and children to hide deep in the deserts of Mexico, in an area known as Chihuahua. Don't you think Geronimo knew the land and the deserts and the way of nature far beyond the imagining of the white man? The white man had their treaty. They had now claimed all of Texas and were busy fighting the Spanish over the borders. Still some tenacious generals couldn't let Geronimo rest. They hunted him; bribed Indians to locate him. His tribe grew. Braves, women, and children all lived the Apache way in hiding. Hidden in the wilderness, their spirit endured like a small flame burning hot. The white man was determined to win. Today they tell the story of Geronimo's capture. Of course, what really went on in 1888, who knows?"

He paused to refill his pipe. *"It was said that a white-haired Indian named Geronimo turned himself in to the authorities, accepting promises of honorary treatment and gifts. Of course, he only did it to protect the tribe. The promises were not kept, and Geronimo was imprisoned until his death. But the Generals' intention was to imprison the spirit of Geronimo. Kill the spirit. A tribe of people going through the motions of existence in a safe haven is not the same. The body becomes a mere shell once the spirit, the spark, the raison d'être is destroyed."*

"You mean you don't think they really got Geronimo?" Mariah asked.

"Well, I don't know if they imprisoned the *real* Geronimo," her father replied, "He could have been a stand-in. But not before he had saved his tribe. We know the government desired something more because they had already taken the land, they had the treaty, yet they wanted the people. They didn't even want their memory to live on. Perhaps those are smart battle tactics, to quell any future rebellion." His voice was almost a mumble now, as if he spoke to himself rather than an audience. "Later, one of the white men excavated the tomb of Geronimo and stole his skull and bones, presumably for the Skull and Bones Society rituals. It was as though they were envious of a power they could never comprehend. It was a bizarre act. It didn't matter which skull, it must be noted that they, in an odd fashion, worship and perpetuate the idea of Geronimo. It has to make you wonder. The question is, did they succeed? Is the Apache way alive and well?" His eyes traveled to each one of his brood as he relit his pipe.

"Huh? Where? You act like you know something," Mariah had said, watching her father closely.

"I have beliefs. Like, '*the meek will inherit the earth*'."

"Who are the meek?" She had asked. The question hung in the darkness.

"*Yes, now that is a question.*" He smiled and looked out into the night as he took a long pull from his pipe.

When she finished the story, the present Mariah looked hard at the velvet darkness as though into the past. She could not see a thing, not with eyes dilated by fire. She shuddered. What had her father been trying to say? What did all this mean? He had tried to make them believe there were Indians all around them in the darkness, hiding.

"Well, I like this Indian story best." Tristan broke her reverie as he stood up and announced, "I'm sleepy now. Will you tuck me in?"

"Yes, dear, of course." Mariah turned to Isabella. "You, too, little one."

David smiled at her.

"First, let's have one more night song," she said, then she put an arm around each of the children and rocked them before the fire. Mariah sang *The Spider Web song,* that no one ever tired of hearing.

CHAPTER 12 *Isabella and the Butterfly*

The next morning, after breakfast, outside with a bin of soapy water set-up on the picnic table, David helped Mariah scrub the sticky camp dishes. Not a drop of food were left on them. Her family was a ravenous bunch. Mariah had made pancakes, no mean feat out in the middle of nowhere, with the wind playing havoc with the flame of their little Coleman cook stove. She used the mix from Pioneer Flour Mills.

"Looks like another perfect day," David said as he dried his hands and slipped them around her waist. She glanced over her shoulder and gave him a suggestive look.

A second later they heard Tristan call out, "I got my fishing rod figured out. I'm going to catch some fish."

Isabella seized the moment, "Tristan, can I come with you? I know how to do it."

"You really want to come, Isabella?"

She nodded her head up and down. Mariah gave David a peck and looked at her daughter. With her hair in braids and her little black moccasins on, Mariah had the urge to hug her. Isabella grinned.

Tristan turned to Mariah. "Okay if she comes, Mom?"

"Yes, if she's ready for such an adventure." Mariah watched her daughter's eager face. "Where are you headed?"

Tristan pointed off to the right. "We'll go down and walk along the bank until the water is deeper."

"That's fine, but keep an eye on your sister." Her hands still wet from the dishes, she crouched down to give each of them a kiss on the cheek.

"You hold this tackle box. Okay Isabella?" Tristan asked.

"Okay." She took it from him, her body tilting to the right with the weight, then trudged behind her brother without complaint.

The two little bodies disappeared into the live oaks and down the narrow path to the stream below.

* * *

"I think we should follow the river a little further because it's too shallow to catch a fish." Tristan eyed his sister, "Do you want to wait here or explore with me?"

"I'm coming with you." Isabella struggled with the box as she trotted to catch up.

"Let's put our stuff by the water. We may have to walk a bit." Tristan set his load down, then keeping his rod, gestured for Isabella to do the same. "Now we each need a walking stick."

She dropped the box and trotted into the woods behind him. They searched until they each found a long branch.

"Now you are ready to be an Indian princess," he said. "But you must be very quiet and tiptoe, because if there is anything out here, we want to see it first."

Isabella flung her long braids over her shoulder; she was prepared for her role. They walked in silence on the soft earth and dried grasses following a path just above the water. Before long, both were itchy with sweat on this Texas summer day.

"Wait." Tristan stuck out his hand to stop his sister. "There's a deep pool. Let's try it. I think I'll put my rod in and if it looks good we'll go back and get the rest of the stuff."

Isabella pointed a chubby finger toward a rock just past Tristan's shoulder. "Oh, look! A butterfly. Can you catch it?"

"Sure can." He turned and swiftly stepped toward the rock, hands outstretched, and then gently enclosed them around the yellow and black winged creature. He held it out to his sister for a moment. They watched the wings open and close, tickling his hand. Then it flew away.

A smile flashed across Isabella's face, then she sighed. "I'm hot and thirsty."

"Splash yourself with some water, but don't drink it. Not here." Tristan sat down on the bank by the water and put his bamboo fishing rod in, while several feet away, Isabella lay down on her belly. She brought the cool water up to her face, careful not to get any in her mouth, then stayed there in the dirt and watched the ants doing their busywork.

Tristan heard a low laugh and twisted around in time to see an Indian, clothed in nothing but a loincloth and a hat of leaves, emerge from the shadows. Raising a finger to his lips, he nodded to Tristan, then motioned for him to stop fishing. Awestruck, Tristan did as he was told, then watched as the Indian lay on the ground and scooted on his belly toward the water. With his swift, soundless movements and funny leaf hat obscuring his face and head, he looked more lizard than human. When he reached the edge of the water, his hand darted out, fast as the speed of light, then drew back clutching a beautiful rainbow-colored fish. He handed the fish to Tristan, who nearly dropped it in his enthusiasm to put it in his bucket. He peered down to examine the fish, but when he looked up to thank the Indian, he had vanished! Tristan looked around, but his new friend was nowhere to be found. That was a good lesson he thought, scratching his blonde head. Unsure what to do, he watched the shiny fish flopping around in his bucket. He looked so sad in there. Tristan was about to free it when the floppy fish wiggled its way out. The grateful creature fell back into the water and slipped into the depths. By this time, Tristan was much more fascinated by the Indian.

"Isabella," he said, "let's walk some more."

Now quite rested, she pulled herself into a sitting position. "Sure. Can we climb those rocks over there?"

"Okay, but stay by me. We don't want to go too high or too far."

They began to climb the white boulders. It looked like some kind of landslide had made them all tumble down into a heap.

"Look, Tristan," Isabella pointed down to a stone that looked different than the rest.

Tristan followed the line of her finger. "Oh, you found a crystal! It's a big one, too."

"It's ginormous." She struggled to break off a small piece of it. "But it's hard and stuck to this rock."

Tristan straightened up. As his eyes searched the cliff face, he saw a dark opening just around the next bend. "Isabella, are you feeling brave?"

She grinned. "I'm the bravest."

"Well, I see a cave. Would you like to go in?"

She nodded and reached up to grab her brother's hand. As they approached the cave, they saw a mix of tall and small boulders scattered about as if guarding the opening. They soon made a game of the hike. Tristan let go of her hand, then climbed on top of a large white boulder and shouted, "I'm the king of the mountain!"

With some effort, Isabella scrambled to keep up. Her golden bronze braids floated out from the bandana. "No, I'm the king of the mountain!" She yelled, as she reached the top.

"Oh! There is a bigger one," Tristan cried. He jumped down, then held out a hand for his sister, and the two continued scrambling from one rock to another.

"Shh," Tristan said. "There's the cave, we're almost there."

Tristan's heart was in his ears. He knew he hadn't imagined that Indian; he must be around here somewhere. He tiptoed over to the wide dark mouth, and jumped back, when a shadow appeared in front of him. His heart thudded when he felt someone tug at his elbow. Isabella was beside him. They got closer, hid their bodies, and peered in. Suddenly a voice said, "Hello."

Tristan froze, then he moved forward, the blood pounded in his head. "Peter?"

"Yes..."

"What are you doing here?"

"I frequently inspect the caves," Peter said.

"Oh, I thought I saw someone and..." Tristan trailed off, not wanting to admit that he'd just been scared half to death. The children stood, their faces in shadow, silhouetted by the sun.

"Come on in, you two. Your eyes will adjust to the darkness."

Tristan and Isabella inched forward. "I've never seen this cave before," Tristan said. After the story his Mom had told last night, he was sure there were Indians somewhere.

"See for yourself. Come on in." They stepped inside and walked around the room-sized shelter. Their eyes slowly became accustomed as they smiled and waited.

"This would be a fine place to live, a good size," offered Tristan.

"Maybe Indians could live in here," Isabella said as she touched her braid.

"All the Indians live on reservations," Tristan said. "You will learn that when you go to school and study Texas history."

Peter grinned. "The last Indian sighting was in 1888, when the Apache's attacked Lakeville. People were surprised because the government had been reining them in to New Mexico by then. That was supposedly the last time they were seen in Texas.

"Well, I think it's very cozy," said Isabella. "I could live here. See, it's a lot bigger than my tent."

"It's cool too." Tristan placed a hand on the wall. "Feel the coolness coming from the walls."

His gaze landed on a huge crystal in the middle of the cave. "Wow, look at that!"

"I see one too!" Shouted Isabella, her voice echoing, *too, too, too*.

They saw a flash of white as Peter smiled at them. "Where are your parents? Do they know you're up here?"

"They're at the campsite. We were fishing, then I noticed this cave from down there and I wanted to explore." Tristan pointed to their spot by the stream.

Peter chuckled, "You remind me of your mother."

"Really?" Asked Tristan "She likes to explore?"

"I've known her for a long time, since she was a teenager. She understands this place."

Isabella was counting. "One, two, three, four. I've counted six crystals in this cave. No seven."

"Do you know what that means?" Peter asked.

"What?"

"You have magic eyes. Crystals are everywhere around here, but not everyone sees them. That's the way this place is."

Tristan's eyes grew wide. Had he imagined that Indian? Had it been a trick of the light?

"Here, I will walk you back." Peter began leading the way out. The three of them bid goodbye to the cave, and once out, squinted into the bright sunlight.

"Peter," Tristan asked, shielding his eyes as he looked up. "Do you mind if I explore the caves around here later?"

"How old are you, boy?"

"Six years old, sir."

"Well then, I think it will be all right. What will you be looking for?"

"Crystals," said Isabella. "I will make my mommy a necklace because I love her very much."

"I'm going to look for Indians," Tristan said.

Peter paused, "Indians?"

"Well, with all those caves, couldn't there be Indians?"

"Tristan, my boy, explore all you want, and if you find any Indians, more power to you. But that will be our secret, okay? Because, if we tell anyone about it, the Indians—if there are any—they might go into hiding."

"Yes, sir."

They stopped at the water to retrieve the fishing pole and tackle box, then finally arrived at the path that led to the campsite. "Oh, there's mom right up there. I guess she's been looking for us. See you later."

Mariah waved from the top as her tired children struggled up the hill to meet her. "Peter," she called out, "will you drop by for dinner later? We have plenty of food."

"Thanks, I'll take you up on that." He turned to the kids and said, "Well guys, my Jeep is the other way. See you kids in a few hours." He slowly strolled away, whistling a vaguely familiar tune.

When she saw her mother, Isabella jumped into her open arms.

"How sturdy and dirty you look," Mariah said as she held her daughter out from her.

"We had fun. We played king of the mountain, we found a crystal palace, and Tristan found a magician in a cave."

"There was a magic butterfly too," said Tristan, "and he told me the secret of eternal youth, so I let him fly away."

"You kids had a great adventure, sounds like." Mariah smiled in relief as she held Isabella to her.

"I have a concept," David said, as they walked back to the campsite on the cliff above two-rivers. "This evening we should all take baths in the waterfall."

"Uooh." The kids scrunched up their faces at the thought.

"Sounds inspired, honey. We must scrub these kids head to toe to see what they really look like. I hardly recognize them," Mariah teased.

CHAPTER 13 *Sunset waterfalls*

Their family was the only visitors to The Ranch. They stood knee deep in the cool spring water near their camp. Mariah had a bowl to pour over Isabella's head as she scrubbed her long hair with Dr. Bronner's peppermint soap. She scrubbed Tristan too, despite his dodging. After the kids were scrubbed clean and busily rinsing, she began to bathe. It felt so natural, a nuclear family standing outside in the golden light of afternoon, bathing. Mariah used the wooden bowl to rinse the soap out of her dark hair. She watched David standing there, totally cool. Water droplets glistened on his tan chest. It seemed natural. Invigorating warmth spread through her body as they tiptoed to the bank and into sandals. Mariah wrapped herself in a towel, then handed one to Tristan and helped Isabella dry off. Then as the two dashed off like a pair of goats, she called to Tristan to watch his sister, and slipped her arm through David's. They strolled back up the hill to their tent. Back at camp she slipped into nice dry jeans and a clean white T-shirt.

"Alone at last," she said as David moved close beside her. "I'm a little chilly."

"I'll warm you up," he said, wrapping his arm around her. She relaxed into the warmth of his body. His firm hands held her. They kissed long. He held her for a moment longer than they should. They could hear the kids musical voices outside the tent.

"Mom, I'm hungry," came Isabella's voice.

"Great," said Mariah as she pulled from David's embrace. "We have a delicious dinner planned. Who wants to help?"

"I do. I do," Isabella offered.

"Let's make the salad together," Mariah suggested.

"I'll gather more wood for the fire," Tristan said, and began gathering kindling at the edge of the woods.

Peter arrived just as Mariah, assisted by Isabel, finished the salad. He had a six-pack in one hand and a bag of fresh peaches in the other.

"Dessert," he said.

"I'm more interested in that," David replied and pointed his spatula toward the beer. He announced that the fish was ready.

After a tasty meal of fresh fish in lots of butter, the five of them gathered around the fire. Mariah noticed that Peter seemed quiet. Tristan sat close to him. How nice, Mariah thought, he was like one of the family. It had always bothered her that Peter hadn't started one of his own. He obviously enjoyed kids

"Peter," she said, trying to draw him out, "this reminds me of that schoolhouse party you had. That was my first time here with my Dad."

Peter smiled a slow smile. "How is Steven these days?"

"He's wonderful. Working on his latest invention—it's a small hot air balloon he rigged to carry his Nikon up in the air. He was striving for the perfect height for a particular shot. The whole apparatus was operated by remote control."

"Sounds like Steven," Peter said, laughing. They continued to talk until the sky was completely dark and the children's eyes drooped with exhaustion. As Peter helped David carry them to their tent, Mariah sat mesmerized by the flames. Talking with Peter reminded her of everything she loved about being out here.

"Guess I'll call it a night," Peter sighed when he and David returned. The faraway look on Peter's face made Mariah wonder if there were trouble in this paradise.

"Everything okay, Peter?"

He paused for a beat. "Yeah, it's nothing. Just some family stuff."

It didn't seem like nothing to Mariah, but although she longed to press him she remained silent. For Peter, who rarely shared anything personal, it had been a significant revelation.

She waved goodbye to Peter. David returned, his face silhouetted by firelight.

"I love you." She spoke quietly as she glanced up at his face.

In the tent Mariah, still tingling from all the spring water, lay on her back, on the soft pile of blankets. She felt fingers slowly walk up her belly and turned her head to see David lying quietly beside her.

"Do I need to check on the kids?" she inquired.

"They're sound asleep," David said.

"And how do you know that?" She turned fully toward him.

"Wild guess." They kissed like a sigh and their bodies embraced the night.

CHAPTER 14 *Fredrick Kiel Story*

The following night, satiated by a big diner, and exhausted from a fabulous day, they all gathered around the fire. Tristan and Isabella's expectant faces glowed in the light.

"We are ready for a story, Mom," Tristan said.

They'd spent the whole day at Jade cove, and hiked to the wall of springs. Mariah and Isabella had enjoyed the glass bottom boat, a new addition. There was a zip-line strung across the lake upon which they all took turns. Tristan had a blast climbing up on the cliff, riding out over the water, and dropping in. Isabella enjoyed riding around in the boat with her Mom. No one was too tired to skip the story. Mariah decided to speak of the early days when the first Settlers had come to Texas.

Mariah remembered Peter's face from the night before when he'd mentioned his family. He had a fantastic family history. As the remnants of stone chimneys and small dwellings and forgotten fences always made Mariah curious, over the years, she'd pieced together quite a tale.

The Fredrick Kiel Story

Fredrick Kiel sat in his rocking chair, puffing his pipe as he stared into the flames. It was late, time to go up to his wife, Helen, who was no doubt, cocooned in a pile of down blankets in their white featherbed.

He was so happy, or content, or pleased with his life. He had left his German homeland and come to Texas to make his fortune. He'd been visiting the local farmers while hunting for the ideal place to build a mill. That had been his focus, in the New Country only a year ago. He nodded his head in amazement. Now he and Helen were expecting their first child. It had been a whirlwind.

He had boldly knocked on the door of the old farmhouse standing brave on the Texas plain. Then when he saw Helen, he was smitten. He liked to think it was all good business, a smart marriage. But she mesmerized him. Everyone knew it.

At the time, he had a good plan, although a sound business sense was his birthright, money not so much. Seeing her that first afternoon had put a fire under him. She took his breath away and amazed him at once. The added bonus was, she had a mind of her own.

Reliving these memories made him realize with a start, that she was upstairs in their second floor bedroom. He tossed another log on the fire, pulled his sweater around him and went upstairs.

He opened the door slowly. The room held a dim glow from the light of a single candle. He blew out the kerosene lantern he held in his hand and tiptoed softly to the washstand to remove his clothes and wash up. She lay sound asleep, her black hair streaming on the white lace pillow, a mountain of cotton blankets piled on top of her. Her book was still in her hand as if she'd just dropped off. For now, it was just the two of them. The two-story farmhouse was large and quiet. Soon, in a couple of months, they would be three. How different life would be, he thought. The pine floor creaked as he stepped to the wardrobe. Helen's eyes opened and she looked around slowly. She stretched her hand out towards him. He hopped into bed. He wrapped his arms about her and kissed her on the lips.

"I have a secret," she mumbled under his warm breath kisses. "I'm dying to tell you."

"I'd" kiss- "love to" –kiss- "hear"- kiss – "all about it." Long kisses as the two embraced in the tangle of feather down.

"Good morning." Helen greeted Fredrick in the sunny kitchen

as he ambled in. The sun streamed in on Helen, who stood by the old stove, one hand on her hip, one leg up on her knee. The other hand flipped pancakes. Her hair flowed down her back in waves. She always brushed it down long before winding it all up on her head. She stifled a yawn as she poured more batter onto the griddle.

"Smells great," Fredrick said. In a moment he was behind her rubbing her tummy. "It's early for you isn't it?" he asked.

"I want to show you my secret finding today."

He set the plates and silverware on the checkered tablecloth. There were already fresh flowers in the cut crystal vase, a wedding present from her cousins. She piled the plates full of pancakes. He ceremoniously pulled the chair for her to sit down.

Fredrick said the blessing.

"When are your parents returning?"

"Next week I think. It's nice when it's just the two of us."

"It's dangerous when it's just the two of us."

"There is a place I know, well let me explain." She buttered her pancakes and poured the warmed maple syrup on the stack. "Our land is a farm, we grow grain, have barns, chickens and horses. You have built a mill. We have plenty of flour for pancakes and biscuits, waffles and tortillas, and bread. My father has worked the land for generations. He is blessed to have good soil. However, Texas is a very great place. It is really still the frontier. So I go on long rides on my horse 'Wildfire'. Just to explore, while you are busy at the mill. You do work such long hours." She smiled. "My mother really runs the house you know. I have had some very long rides out into the territory.

"Now with the baby almost three months due, the doctor said I shouldn't ride anymore." She stopped abruptly. "That's my secret."

"That's a good secret," Fredrick spoke slowly. "I am quite surprised. I hope you haven't been lonely?" He reached for her hand and she held his eyes as he held it.

Then she moved quietly over to him and he held her. The smell of coffee filled the silence. It was a big sacrifice for his feisty bride to hold still. Only the beginning of the many changes that would come with a family he knew. The wind knocked on the door. These calls came with the open prairie upon which their farm dwelt. She resumed her seat and dug into the pile of pancakes. Then noting Fredrick's cup was almost empty, Helen got up to refill his cup. When she sat back down across from him, he noticed the sparkle in her eye.

"What's up?"

"I would like us to go out to the territory together by carriage. Have a two or three day trip and go further than I have been able to go alone."

"Why that's all? Of course we could."

"It's very beautiful land, full of clear rivers and deep canyons. We could explore the canyons together. I'd like to show them to you."

"Do you have a goal?"

"No. I mean I can't go far enough alone. With the Indians around and all. This is still the frontier, although we live near a town. The further out you go, the terrain is quite different. Quite beautiful. It reminds me of something, you see."

He didn't see. But he wanted to, he was curious about both; his new wife, and what made her tick, and Texas.

As they talked, they finished eating and she stacked the dishes. He carried them to the sink. He followed her out to the yard as she strolled past the picket fence to the chickens roost. "It's quite different." She began collecting eggs. "I can't explain it. I've lived here all of my life, and I had never ventured out that way before. I just have a feeling. There is a small settlement near there. Not quite a town, Lakeville."

"Frederiksberg is the biggest town for miles." Fredrick agreed.

"The village has a dance hall, I think. I have only heard mention of it. I'm curious to go."

"Wait. The Indians were seen in that area just last month? I read about it," Fredrick said.

"Huh. This is their land first. My grandmother is Indian, you know, of the tribe called Apache." Helen touched her dark glossy hair.

"I didn't realize," Fredrick said. "That's why you ride so well."

"But my Mother is pure German." She stomped her foot. "Anyway we could stay there, spend the night, and explore during the day."

"Why not?" He said. "When your parents return we'll go. If I hadn't been exploring America, I would never have found you in the first place. Here I am in Texas and I have barely been out of Frederiksberg. You are right to check out the territory."

A week later, the young couple headed out. They traveled by a two horse carriage, Fredrick working hard to make sure she was comfortable. In their hearts they both knew that once they had a little one they would be more grounded. He didn't want her to feel trapped. His Helen was a force of nature. She moved with purpose attacking all she did with gusto. He endeavored to help with the baby when he arrived. He'd married her young. Her parents had given consent and welcomed him, as she was quite mature for her age. He hoped she would speak up always, like she was now, and not ever feel her life with him to be a burden. She seemed to express a vague longing for a place she hadn't even seen, a place beyond the horizon.

Once they arrived in the town, they settled in to the only Inn.

"Yes, I am happy." She answered his worried expression.

He put his hand on her belly and felt the sudden kick.

"He's happy too," she smiled. Then she settled in to sleep on the huge pile of pillows on the high feather bed at the Lakeville Inn.

Her eyes were closed and she was already dreaming. She dreamed of fields and steep hills, rocky dry land—endless hills, scrubby trees, fragrant cedars, and so many huge rocks. An old woman with long grey braids wound on top of her head, dressed in black, with a black shawl draped over her shoulders came to her. She advanced slowly. A huge black bird flew in the sky above her shoulder. The sky was completely white, the air held a chill. The woman came closer and closer headed straight for her. Helen stared into the soft grey eyes. The eyes were so wise. Not a word was spoken.

Then she woke up. That morning, Helen begged her husband to let her ride. "If you are with me, I will be safe. There are no roads going back into the territory."

Fred was surprised to learn how far his wife had traveled in a day by horseback. As they rode their mounts at a peaceful steady walk, Helen peered around as though searching. They crossed shallow rivers and climbed up rocky banks. Helen had let her black hair down. As she rode ahead, up hills peering across the landscape, and back down, he realized how like an Indian she looked. She preferred not to ride sidesaddle, and he didn't complain. She just wore her pantaloons and her high-laced boots. Her skirt removed and tucked into the saddlebags. She was a free spirit. They stopped to let the horses drink and graze at a fragrant meadow. They tethered the two mounts to a tree and pulled a pack lunch from the saddlebags.

Helen seemed to relish laying flat on her back, staring up at the sky. Fredrick pulled out his pipe from his breast pocket and watched her as he smoked. She seemed content to watch the birds fly. She wandered around, picking wild flowers and making braided chains, almost as thought he weren't there. Fredrick was often intrigued by all she didn't say. The territory was isolated and endlessly quiet.

Mounting again,they rode on. Occasionally they saw a homestead, or a goat farmer, but they just waved and rode on by. He didn't know what she was seeking. He was certain she would know when she found it. Though Helen wasn't a talker, her eyes betrayed a face that masked a mystery. He didn't like to press, so he let her have her thoughts. Wondering what she was thinking, he entertained himself on the long rides into the wilderness. When he observed his wife much later having tea with the society ladies, he could watch her eyes behind her polite expression and knew she was remembering their special times together.

After each full days ride, they headed back to the inn for a late supper. Helen's face glowed and her eyes sparkled. Thank you, was all she would say. Her happiness filled his heart.

Helen awoke with a start into the grey dawn slashed with an orange streak of early morning rays. She'd had the dream again. This would be their last day. She knew Fredrick would have to return to work. She must succeed now, because any later she would be too pregnant to mount the horse. Once again they saddled up and rode out after a small breakfast of ham and biscuits prepared by the Innkeepers wife.

When they passed by the homesteads, she noticed the people looked old and haggard. The gardens were wilted and the scrawny chickens scratched the dirt. Why are they so isolated from each other? Helen thought. It seemed like a lonely existence.

The rhythm of the ride lulled her into a deep relaxation. And then her eye caught the silver sliver of a tributary off the main river they had passed by just the day before. She signaled to Fredrick who followed behind at a steady pace. She ducked her head under a low limb from a live oak tree and followed the trail up along the upper path next to a huge green lake. As they came down the other side of the smooth, jade colored expanse of water, they once again followed the stream. It was wider here. The canyon walls were steep and towered high on both sides. Again she heard a hawk scream and looked up, watching the bird ride the airwaves.

It slowly dawned on Fredrick as he watched his wife, why they always rode in silence. His Helen was watching, listening, following some unknown guidance. She was deeply tuned in to the wild nature out here. This was fascinating to him. It seemed her very being, resonated with the land. Abruptly she stopped, swung down off her horse, Wildfire, and tethered him to a small pecan tree by the rivers edge. She waited completely impatiently for him to dismount and tie his horse. He hurried towards her before she could stomp her foot or something. She reached for his hand and pulled him towards her, she planted his hand on her waist as she turned and began to climb fast up the canyon wall. Such a lady he thought he'd married. He shook his head. He had to scramble fast before she left him in the dust.

Now she was on a ledge of some kind. She paced to and fro inspecting the back wall.

"See? It's like a cave only its enclosed on three sides. It doesn't have an entrance into the cliff. But look!" Helen said.

He looked. There were all these complicated pictures and markings. Symbols painted in black and red, like cave paintings. This must be so old.

"How ancient is this place?"

"I don't know what to think, but I do think this is what I have been searching for." Helen was dumfounded. "Do you know what it is?"

"It's like ancient cave paintings, but that predates history," Fredrick said. "It predates the Egyptians. It's like hieroglyphics but not as sophisticated. This could be over 5,000 years old."

Helen looked out and far from this spot. "5,000 years old. How? What? And yet there is no one living out here for miles."

Fredrick shook his head. Who is this magic woman he is married to? What would his sons be like? I shall always listen to her dreams and visions. He vowed silently, then and there.

They had meandered for miles each day, all to find their way to this spot. Helen had known she would find something remarkable. It seemed once she had spotted the tributary, she had made a beeline to this place. The whole ride felt magical. This huge canyon was somehow very special. Helen sat down and studied the marks and symbols for a long while. There were marks that looked like buffalo, stick figures of men, other circles and shapes, and wavy lines. All were either black like charcoal or an iron oxide color.

Fredrick's mind was so full of the miracle that he forgot for once to smoke his pipe.

Once they were back at the Inn, they had a late supper.

"We only have a half-day trip to reach Frederiksberg tomorrow. You can sleep as long as you like in the morning." Fredrick smiled down at his wife.

Helen awoke once and glanced around startled in the strange room. She groped for her husband's large warm hand in the dark. She clutched it until she fell back asleep. Fredrick turned toward his wife and wrapped his arms around her.

With the morning light just breaking through the clouds, they rode in the carriage back towards Frederiksberg. *They picked up the week's supplies at the general store on the way home.*

* * *

"To be continued," Mariah whispered. She at once remembered her Dad the moment she said those words. There was a moment of dead silence with only the rustling sound of low burning coals.

"Wow, Mom, don't stop now," Tristan said.

"It's late, way past your bedtimes, even my bedtime."

"That's an awesome story, Mom."

"It's true."

"Is that here? At the Ranch?"

"Yes of course it is! We will hike all the way to the cave paintings tomorrow."

"Is Helen like an Indian?" Tristan asked.

"She is part Indian," Mariah said.

"Are you? You have long black hair."

"No. I'm not, you know I'm French. You met my Gramma Yvonne," Mariah said. "Well, maybe in spirit. Go to sleep now so you will be ready. It's a long hike in the morning."

David helped Tristan, and Mariah gathered up Isabella into her arms, and they bundled them into the orange pup tent that was just their size. Mariah liked best to spend an entire day at each place the Ranch offered. She was now especially excited to revisit the cave paintings her sister Kristen and she had found so long ago.

CHAPTER 15 *Blue Spring*

"I like being married," David said the next morning as he poured cereal into a bowl. A sleepy haze covered the valley below in the dim light of dawn.

"That's a good thing," Mariah smiled at him. She loved him out here—away from all the pressure of young-married-couple poverty. Their life in the city was tense. They both were exhausted from working all day and not sure if it would be enough to cover the bills and leave something left over. Yet, out here, they had only to listen to the whispers of the river and look into the eyes of their children to know that they were blessed. They had married for better or worse, richer or poorer.

She remembered the time she had been at a party, dancing with a wealthy Houston lawyer. She had told him what she did for a living. Someone had told him that David, her husband, was an artist.

"Two poor people married to each other," the guy had clucked. "What a shame." He had shaken his head as if it was the worst fate to befall a couple. He was thinking about The Good Life and all its pleasures, but Mariah was not fazed. She had never dreamed of those things in the first place. She had then danced a slow song with David, and what a wonderful dance that was. She laid her head on his strong chest. His arms held her close. She studied the crowd. The mayor of Houston was there, with different who's-who dressed in their sequins and shiny shoes. People clinked their cocktails and cackled, but really the make-up crinkled in the folds of their skin. She noted everyone looked old and tired. Their smiles painted in place. But she, in a simple white sundress that made her bronze tan glow and David, with his blue eyes smiling at her as they enjoyed the slow dance together, they were a team. Now she looked at David and thought, if only life were just dances and camping.

She looked at him now, unshaven and sleepy-eyed, she reached over and tossed his unruly curls, then she threw her arms around him a bit dramatically. Oh hell she was dramatic anyway. He reached over his shoulder and pulled her onto his lap.

"Having fun yet?" He gleamed at her.

She nodded. "Coffee tastes good out here."

After breakfast, David piled everyone into the four-wheeler. Mariah hopped in last with the basket of fruit and snacks she had put together, along with a few refillable water bottles. The kids had loaded in the towels and air mattresses. They took the pretty drive along the mossy path beside a shallow stream lined with sycamores. As they rounded the last bend and crossed the shallow stream the sight took Mariah's breath away. The shear bone white boulders framed an intense waterfall that gushed forth into a crystal blue pool of pristine water. David parked the jeep and everyone jumped out.

Again, as it was the middle of the week, they were the only people out here for miles. The shear isolation was part of the magic. It was almost ten am. and already stinging hot. The kids clamored over ouchy hot rocks to the waters edge. Mariah put the towels and supplies on the large boulders they would relax on after the swim.

As she inched her bare feet into the icy water her legs went numb. She looked up; David had already climbed up the waterfall on the far side of the pool. The pool was almost round with a 30-foot diameter and over 30 feet deep. She put the water wings on Isabella before she charged in. Icy water could take your breath away. Tristan ran on in after David. Before she could stop her, Isabella chased him right in, splashing and bobbing up and down in the spring. Mariah was frozen in place watching. Slowly she inched forward as legs, hips and thighs grew numb. She knew once she ducked her head under she would be fine.

Soon they were all swimming. David beat everyone up to the top and made a perfect swan dive from the twelve-foot cliff. Mariah played with Isabella, who swam back and forth towards the frothing waterfall. David showed Tristan the rope wedged into rocks at the falls. Soon, Tristan too, was on the top of the cliff. Mariah was content to swim with Isabella while the boys never tired of jumping in and climbing back up. Mariah blew up the air mattresses and both she and Isabella got on and floated around the edges, peering into the deep as far as the eye could see. She could see light through the water to lime green fronds swaying in the current. Golden and silver fish swam far below. The sunlight pierced the water and shone circles on the rocky bottom. Isabella was spellbound watching the scene in this world beneath the water.

"You are a little Mermaid."

"I want to take the water wings off."

"I know you are a good swimmer, but the water's too cold. It can take your breath away if you go under. It's a safety thing."

"OK."

"You can see a lot through the water while we float on top."

"Yes, I want to go down there."

"It's better up here."

Later, as they perched on the boulders they warmed up in the sun.

While on dry land the kids wore water shoes to protect from the sharp rocks and wood debris. Tristan had now joined David to jump from the highest part of the cliff. Isabella was content to dry off and play with the rocks and shells. When Mariah looked back for her daughter, she had disappeared. She searched the area and spotted her half way up a cliff. She recited her moms quote from The Prophet, "You are the bows from which your children, as living arrows, are sent forth.' She therefore stayed her distance as she went to follow, curious and watchful. She watched her daughter climb, sure-footed as a goat. Nature was a good teacher. They all felt safe out here.

"Look at me," shouted Tristan, as he jumped from the high rock. She watched as he splashed a big cannonball splash and kept her eyes on the spot until he surfaced. She breathed a big sigh of relief. Then she scrambled the rest of the way up the hill to join Isabella who didn't seem to have any intention of stopping any time soon.

"Lets go down together, its time for a swim," Mariah said. She knew sometimes the mistakes happened on the way down—not the way up. "You can get over confident and a rock could slip out from beneath your feet."

Once they were back on the rocky shore, Mother and daughter jumped in the spring water and swam towards the rushing waterfall.

David belongs in the country, Mariah was convinced, as she watched him back at camp, after the kids were back in the pup tent. He's like a pioneer, living on his wit and strength and his knowledge of the wild. As if on cue, his hand snaked around her shoulder and approached her breast. Laughing, she smacked the offending hand away. How she wished they could stay here, among the grass and trees and youthful memories that seemed to come alive under the starry Texas sky. "You are not a tame city boy!"

CHAPTER 16 *Helen's Story*

Once again, after a dinner of skillet fried potatoes, burgers, and hotdogs, there was a wonderful peace around the campfire. Flames danced high into the pitch-black air, as darkness tried to swallow the fire. Tristan and Isabella looked cozy in their footie pajamas.

"Mom, Mom, tell us a story," Tristan and Isabella clamored.

"Again?" Mariah said. Truly she was inspired to continue the tale.

"Yes, we want to know what happens," Isabella said.

Mariah was glad to carry on the family tradition. She told her children of the old grandmother with the crow on her shoulder that had appeared in her dreams, when she slept at The Ranch.

"Wow Mom, I'm scared." Isabella said.

"Are you for real?" Tristan asked.

"Listen carefully, and I will tell you a tale." Mariah's voice was slow and deep. The inky darkness fueled her imagination, and she continued.

The Fredrick Kiel Story

Seven years later find Helen and Fredrick blessed with many children. There were five born after the first-born boy. They moved to San Antonio where Fredrick expanded his highly successful Mill operation. Helen oversaw the construction of the stately mansion they built in the Garden District. Fredrick insisted on importing many things from Europe. Huge fireplace mantels, stately columns for the front porch, Italian tile, and German chandeliers were all hand-picked on their trips to Europe.

Helen's home was soon full of the loud boisterous shouts and games of healthy children.

"It's the weekend tomorrow. Are things running smoothly at the mill?" she asked one evening.

"Of course, my queen. Smooth as usual, bumpy as usual. One thing after the next, but isn't it all so interesting." Fredrick grabbed Fred as he chased after Mary who had swiped his cap and tossed it to Amy. "How is my boy?" He tossed him up in the air to squeals of delight.

"Me too, me too!'

"What's up?" Fredrick turned to Helen.

"I had another dream. The old woman came again. It's a sign. It's my sign to visit the Frontier again."

"Shall we buy some land there?"

"Ah well, we have this fine estate here in San Antonio, and my parents still have the farm in Frederiksberg."

"That is all quite useful, my little Dusseldorf."

"This land is different. No one can own the frontier."

"It cannot be farmed?"

"It cannot be tamed. It is just land for lands sake. No one should ever own these vast expanses of land. How can one person own it? That seems crazy. All these Europeans trying to own America."

Young Freddie, only four, was by the door listening to his parents. Fredrick puffed his pipe and loaded it again. "Yes, I see."

It was a golden afternoon in the large solid brand new house.

They had planned the layout together and then worked with the Architect. They had considered every detail of their lifestyle: entertaining, business, and living day to day. They liked to live where they worked. So they wanted a house to be functional and practical, a beautiful place for their large growing family. Helen was from a farm family. Farmers always did that. You didn't go to work; work was a way of life. It was around you. Although in town, the estate encompassed several acres.

They loved being out of doors and sunlight. So the house was full of light—large windows, sun-rooms, garden rooms, and morning rooms with thin shear curtains at the windows. Helen with her oldest children had designed elaborate mosaic patterns to be installed in the kitchen. Helen had suggested the idea of wheat bundle designs for the kitchen fireplace mantel. The Architect made formal drawings from her sketches for the cabinetmaker.

Fredrick spared no expense in buying the finest materials or ordering them from Europe if they weren't available in Texas.

Helen was pleased, content, and happy. Her daughters played the piano and her sons took drawing lessons. She was active and busy in their lives and her own.

And now the dream. The dream was a blessing and a curse. It shook the status quo. She wasn't to just be *content*. It boded of something more. Something she must do—was compelled to do. She loved the dreams especially now, because she was a woman in society. But this was her secret. Only Fredrick and her family shared this. The old woman reminded her of the spirit of her youth and her adventurous nature. The unexplored Frontier was not dangerous to her, but her place of peace. A place of solitude. A glimpse at the magnificence of this great Country.

"Shall we bring all of the children for a stay in the country?" Fredrick's voice broke her reverie.

"Oh, yes." She dropped her knitting in her haste to run to her husband like a youth and kiss his cheek. "There is something about the dream this time. As if there is a secret. With all the children we can explore even further."

So they packed up the whole brood and went by carriage to the Texas Hill country town. When they got to Lakeville they heard there had been an Indian raid. Almost all of the supplies were gone. "I thought they were peaceful Indians. All the goat farmers out here always minded their own business. But Geronimo is on the loose." Fredrick read from the newspaper. "He is supposedly hiding in Mexico somewhere. And all the Indians are on edge. The government has been herding them all up."

"Herding!" Helen was incensed. "They are not animals. This is their country for heaven's sake."

Fredrick glanced firmly at his wife. There were so many newcomers. And half of them Europeans, who mistook the natives for savages.

"Yay, Geronimo," Helen muttered softly under her breath.

Young Freddie heard that.

She smiled demurely at the Innkeeper, small towns had sharp ears.

"We'll stay two nights," Fredrick told the Innkeeper.

The Innkeeper's wife fawned over all of the kids and how they had grown. With the help of the Innkeeper's son, they unloaded all of their bags and settled in to their rooms.

After all of the years of exploration, they had found their favorite place to go. They borrowed seven horses from the Innkeeper and packed a picnic. After lunch they headed out down the back roads and creek draws that lead to their familiar haunts. They crossed four low water streams, the water clear as glass. They climbed the cliffs to a high point that overlooked the valley and the rushing brook. It was green and moss covered. There they tied up the horses. The youngest had to ride with his Dad. All the others had their own horses. This particular spot was a large meadow with an open clearing. There were small homesteads scattered around. This particular spot was quiet and unoccupied. The locals had gotten used to their family escapades here. After a picnic they walked the horses quietly along the riverside. They rode for several miles before they came to a huge green lake. They tied up the horses in the shade. All the children undressed and dove right in, swimming hard and fast to keep warm in the icy water. Fredrick stepped out of his clothes revealing a red and white striped suit beneath, that looked a bit like long johns. He dove in neatly and began doing the backstroke. Helen was modest as she prepared for her swim. Soon they were all playing n the water. They pointed up river to the springs. What's up there?

"Just the one thousand springs that fill this lake."

The water was so clear you could see the fish. They never fished. Just delighted in the crystal clear cold freshness of the magic water. No work, the plan was to play and be one with nature. That was the goal. Pack it in. Pack it out.

"Mom do you mind if we go?"

"Go?"

"Follow the shallow tributary?"

"Of course you can. We come here to explore after all."

So the young ones played in the small bathtub sized pools of water. And the older ones climbed the cliffs. Helen and Fredrick strolled arm and arm to the fresh water wall of springs and drank their fill. Little Freddie noticed his father did seem older than his Mom who had the grace of a young doe. But he knew she was devoted to him and to them.

Hours later, the two older boys, Harold and Karl came back. "We found something, Come. Come with us." They yanked at their father's hand.

"We study art history at lessons but I have never seen anything like this."

Helen was proud her boys could make the discovery on their own. The find was more powerful that way. The whole family then trooped to look at the new discovery. The young boys scrambled to the top first. Then they held out there hands to help their sisters and Mom. Once upon the cliff, Helen stared past the cliff. She looked to the top, above where they were standing. She saw someone. She was sure it was a figure. There was a movement, just at the edge of her vision, then it was gone. She felt a presence too. She clutched Fredrick's hand and stared with the full fierceness of her vision. She saw nothing but cactus silhouetted against the sun. But she knew someone was there. She focused back on her children. But her feet barely touched the ground.

"Yes?"

"These paintings. They are symbols like Egyptian Hieroglyphics. See?" Karl said.

They were symbols, painted in faded red or blood brown and scratched into the stone. They seemed Ancient. A mixture of symbols, figures, and animals. None of them knew what it meant.

"This must be Native cave paintings. Can you tell the date?" Helen asked. "Do you think they could be 5,000 years old? Prehistoric?"

"I'm not a scientist yet, Mom," Karl said. "But I know there are scientific methods for dating things."

"That's fantastic." Helen glanced at the floor of the cave-like interior. There were the remains of a fire. "I wonder if the settlers ever come back here? These farmers we've met seem a little old and preoccupied with farming. Eking out a living from the earth and hard toil. Perhaps," she mused, "it's like a message from the past, on these walls, in this terrain." Helen glanced up at her sons. "I love our discoveries."

"Do you and Dad plan to buy some land out here?" Karl asked.

"Buy it? Why who owns it? We can visit, but not own." She looked all around at the serenity of the place. "This land must be free to just be. For the sake of itself. Not to farm or extract monetary gain. Or remove her bounties."

"You mean like the gold diggers out west?" he asked.

"Yes, precisely," Helen said. "Anyway it's the water supply for the entire region. Every farmer deserves access to the miracles of this land." And more than just the farmers, she was sure, but didn't say. "Come children," she said as she opened her arms.

They all sat around her in a semi-circle. "Let's sit together and thank God for making such a beautiful earth and such bounty upon her. Thank him for showing us the way to find such beauty and peace on his sacred day."

"Thank you, God for a mother who takes us on such fun adventures," said Little Freddie.

"Thank God for our parents and this beautiful country," said Harold.

"Thank you for the soul of ancient man who creates such gorgeous paintings for us to find in our modern time," Amy said. "He has sent us a message through the ages."

"Let's all bow our heads in a silent prayer." Fredrick said.

"Thanks for taking us. Its been way to long," Helen said.

This place seemed to lend itself to prayer. They felt safe and secure out here. Helen was grateful they had come. She was certain this is what the old lady in the dream had wanted her to see. She wondered about what she had seen above the cliff. She didn't want to alarm the children. She wasn't even sure if she should tell her husband. He was so prominent in society now. Could he relate? Would he understand?

They looked up and grinned at one another. The kids scrambled off to explore the caves that were tucked into the cliff side. The little ones threw rocks down to the valley below. Fredrick lit his pipe.

Helen began to pace about in circles. When no one was watching she hiked up her skirts exposing her high-laced boots. Then she scaled the cliff to the top. No one followed, as all were preoccupied. She pulled herself up and over the top with her strong arms. She ignored the few scrapes she got doing it. Once on top, an amazing site greeted her. She had reached a large plain that stretched as far as the eye could see. A plateau.

All day they had been hiking in a huge canyon, etched by time and water. She had been expecting a sort of hilltop. Not this vast expanse. The wind blew strong up here. It was already late afternoon but the sun shone bright. She noticed a worn bit of path in the dirt and decided to follow it. Feeling suddenly like the brave teen-age girl she'd been once upon a time. It's as if the land revealed its secrets slowly. Always revealing something new, each time she came. A sharp sound in the brush startled her. She turned her head; it was a large shy deer. The deer stared straight at her for a few seconds and then bounded away. Helen stood stock still on this hint of a path, unsure if she should move. Then she did. Carefully placing one foot in front of the other. She was wearing moccasins and tread ever so quietly towards a lone scrubby gnarled oak tree. She followed the path straight into the brush. She moved closer, following an azure light. It opened to a clearing. In the center of a sandy circle her eyes focused on a fire. Then she realized there was a ring of ten or so teepees scattered around.

An old wise woman approached, pointed her finger and beckoned her come. Helen heeded this summons and stepped forward. The wind blew her hair, and she was aware that it was no longer coiled atop her head, but floating freely around her. She followed the woman into one of the teepees. Once inside, she was greeted by two women. Together they carefully removed her dress and gave her an Indian white leather one to wear. They put her dress outside to dry by the fire. She sat cross-legged with them on a woven rug. The two older women were soon joined by two younger ones. They bowed, nodded a greeting, but did not speak. They passed a wooden bowl filled with golden liquid around the circle. Helen took the drink gratefully, suddenly very thirsty. The liquid was warm and sweet, yet unlike anything she had ever tasted. The old woman gestured for her to stand. She appeared so similar to the stout woman that came in her dreams. Helen arose and followed them single file out of the tent. Everything on the plateau was now etched in twilight gold. Four Indian braves stood in a row. She stooped through the flap as she came out toward them. She ran her hands down the soft white buckskin of her dress. It was beaded with seed pearls and the fringes tickled her bare calves.

Once she joined them by the fire, someone drew a circle around her feet. Each Indian placed a small gift in four points around the circle. One was a small leather pouch. One was a bowl of grain. The other was a small antler. The last maiden placed a white flower in the circle. The eldest brave lifted her face to his. He then touched her shoulders and her forehead with a special pollen he held in his hand. Finally, he placed his soft lips in the middle of her forehead like a kiss. Then still holding her shoulders he gazed straight into her eyes. But he was looking into, and beyond her. As if there were some hidden depth or meaning to her. Something she herself wasn't quite aware of.

I am Geronimo, he told her without words. Mind to mind. This is my home. It has been my grandfather's home and his grandfather's home before him. This is the only land where no one comes. It is sacred, and it is protected. I have traveled far from the cage that they wanted to trap me and my tribe in. I have brought my family here. This is my son Naiche. My wife has tended you. All around us are my tribe. We have traveled far. We will stay here. He nodded with finality as if this should explain everything. Helen looked all around as far as the eye could see. She looked both down to the earth and up into the amber sky and she knew his home was a very big place. He must be referring to land as far as he could run in a day—in every direction.

Helen smiled with a kind of triumph in her heart.

"And the dream?" She asked with her eyes.

"Your grandmother. She was my wife. Our children were stolen by settlers when she was murdered. I had a baby boy."

My father, she thought. Tears welled in her eyes. Geronimo's hair was white, but he was still strong. "This is the Indian maiden ceremony. You are a brave maiden."

She smiled as she thought after six kids was she still a maiden?

"As you were raised by the white man, you have missed this ceremony."

She threw her arms about him.

Then she turned to all of the others. One by one she greeted them.

Then seeing the timid sliver of moon arise in the sky, she returned to the teepee. There they removed her dress. She put her own heavy pioneer garb back on. She left them one of her petticoats as a gift, sorry she didn't have more to give. She solemnly hugged each of the women goodbye. She walked backwards away from their tent until the woods swallowed her up into their embrace. She turned and ran back to the spot above the cliff, from whence she had come.

When Helen grew close, she slowed. She peaked over the edge. Two young girls were sitting down below wearing almost nothing— little brightly colored floral panties and small tops. Momentarily shocked, she stepped back. Then looked again. There was no one there. She could hear her husband's voice calling. Calmly she descended the cliff.

"Hello my little explorer, glad you have returned to us." Fredrick patted her affectionately. He glanced at the now fading light of the sky overhead. Twilight was settling in, with a sliver moon etched like a gentle line into the blue. A cool wind blew her skirt. She glanced down quickly to her daughter. She looked into the dirty stained face with such deep brown eyes. Serious eyes. "Do you like it?" Her daughter asked.

"Yes. What?"

"See, I found an arrowhead. Look it's so large."

"Its wonderful honey. Just wonderful." She took her daughter's hand in hers.

"The boys headed back already," Fredrick explained.

The three of them, arm in arm, walked back along the river towards the lake. All were quiet. When they reached the lake, the boys had already started a campfire. The light warmed them and the cedar smelled so good.

"Tonight we can camp here," Fredrick Kiel said. "Tomorrow night we can have a more civilized stay at the Inn." He nodded to the horses, tethered to the trees, and peacefully grazing.

"Yay!" They all shouted.

Mariah glanced over at her sleepy children. Even David seemed touched by the story.

"I'm glad someone decided to buy the ranch," Tristan said.

"So am I. I'm glad Peter's friends with my dad and we can bring you guys out here," Mariah said.

"Now he's our friend," Tristan said. " I like him, Mom."

"I know, me too," she said.

"Me too!" Isabella rubbed her eyes.

Together, they gathered them up, Isabella over David's shoulder and Mariah took Tristan's hand. Soon they were tucked in to sleeping bags and down pillows. The first time Mariah had heard the story about Peter's grandmother, Helen, she wanted to know more. She could never quite get it out of her head. She resonated with this land like Helen had. Thank god Peter seemed to understand her and her special connection to this place. Helen's deep connection had to be explained—her being part Indian inspired Mariah to embroider the facts. Helen had recognized a kindred soul in her great-grandson, Peter. That is why he was the land steward of this rock strewn majestic place.

"Mom, are you talking about our cliff paintings? Tristan asked. "The very same ones?"

"Yes, honey."

" Wow, they're that old?"

"Indeed they are, much older in fact," Mariah whispered, smiling.

CHAPTER 17 *Leaving*

Later the following day, sooner than anyone was ready to, it was time to embark on the long drive back to Houston. Mariah didn't know why they had to pack-up at noon on the hottest part of 105% day. But she was grateful they had stayed until the very last minute, and all had a morning swim at Jade Cove before packing up. Now the car was loaded and the campsite was immaculate. No sign humans had invaded the place for a few days. The fire was out.

They all clamored into the Suburban and David revved the engine. They hadn't driven anywhere for days. Peter always let them borrow the jeep for traversing the property. David pulled out and drove down the tight grass-dirt path that served as a road. In the meadow, he lurched to a stop.

"What? Flat tire? I hadn't even noticed it. It must have been a slow leak," David said, dismayed. "OK, everybody out."

Mariah began unloading all of the gear stuffed in the back so they could retrieve the spare tire. She smiled at David as they worked in tandem. "I wish we had one of my dads camping boxes. I see now why he invented it."

"You get your wish, we get to stay longer."

"Ha, ha," Mariah said.

The kids clamored up on a rock and began to play cats-cradle while the parents changed the tire.

"I bet Peter has air at the barn, we can fill up the spare back at his house. It should hold us until the next town."

Tristan crouched on his knees behind the back wheel, as his dad jacked up the rear. He pointed at a huge scorpion that came crawling out of the wheel well. Isabella hoped off the rock to inspect his find. The creature was huge and evil with sharp pincers. Mariah kept her distance, peeking over David's shoulder. They all turned, when Peter pulled up in his Blue jeep.

"Hey guys, glad I caught you. Just wanted to drop bye and thank you for dinner. I brought a watermelon."

"Thanks, we were planning to stop by on our way out," Mariah said. "We had a little mishap."

"I see that."

"And Tristan spotted this scorpion."

Peter crouched down beside the tire to look. "I've never seen one so huge. It's dangerous, stay back." Peter ordered. "I'll take care of it. Let me grab my gun."

Isabella shrieked in horror. "Don't kill the poor creature."

"I'm serious, it's poisonous. Back away." Peter was firm. "Let me give you a hand with that David. You can air the spare up back at the barn."

Mariah grabbed the watermelon and headed to the picnic table. She pulled out her trusty pocketknife, and sliced it up for the kids. Hungry already after such excitement, they dug in.

Grateful, Mariah took a big bite. The ice-cold melon was just what they needed before the long drive. While both kids were enjoying the fruit, and spitting seeds out at each other, Peter took care of the creature with his heavy workman's boot. Of course, after they ate all of the watermelon, tossing the rind off behind the bushes for the wild life, Peter offered David a beer. Mariah cheered with her last slice, as she never drank the stuff.

"Well, we're off after a great visit."

Peter offered each kid an arrowhead. "Don't forget this place," he said solemnly. Mariah recognized the box he kept on the mantle.

"Goodbye Peter. Thanks again for everything." Mariah hugged him goodbye.

"Have a good trip. Drive safe," Peter cautioned, as if he was sending a child into a dangerous world.

"I hope we see you again soon. It's been awesome," David said.

"Thanks for everything. We'll be back." Tristan shook his hand.

"Well, you better." Peter grinned.

The family drove in silence. Peace and exhaustion permeated their subdued faces. Mariah felt thrilled and excited all over.

Isabella said, "I'm sleepy Mama. Can I sit in your lap?"

"Sure, hon, come on. I made sun tea in these gallon jugs, sweetened with honey. Would you like some?"

Isabella settled in her mother's arms. "Not now, I'm so sleepy."

She's such a big three-year-old, Mariah thought, as she felt the warm, soft weight of her younger child. Just last spring I was nursing her. She's healthy and independent, with a strong spirit and a real mind of her own. Mariah loved that she still liked to snuggle like a baby, even if it was only when she was tired.

"You're such a good swimmer. And brave to jump in that icy cold water," she told her, but Isabella was already dozing.

They nodded good-byes to the buck in the woods along the road, and the wild turkey, and the few Jack rabbits they saw scurry along the path. "It's one hundred degrees out here," David said, as he drove. The heat had settled a silence on this crew, along with the sleepiness a bright afternoon sun brings, when it slants through the windows.

Something Peter had said by the fire last night, replayed in Mariah's head. "Do you ever go to Houston?" she'd asked him, thinking she'd return the hospitality. He'd shaken his head. "Been there once and I've never had any desire to go back. That's plenty for me." She had pondered that; contentment in life so great that you didn't want anything. No desire for museums, or culture, or society. A big city, with all the bells and whistles of modern life, held nothing for Peter. I guess he really is a hermit, she thought. For all its stresses, she did love the city. The downtown was new and grand, with a seemingly endless calendar of festivals, art, and music events. There were restaurants and parties, dance clubs—and Mariah did love to dance. The Ranch, by contrast, seemed like a monk's existence to her, pure isolation in a vast hunk of nature.

The kids had fallen asleep hours ago, and there was a peaceful hum in the car. The dark miles slipped by as David drove.

"We got a late start leaving," Mariah said. "It's super late now."

"It's fine. No traffic," David said. "How about a song?"

So David and Mariah sang some Peter, Paul, and Mary folk tunes, another of her family traditions. She had learned all of the words when her Mom and Dad used to sing them together. Then they tried to make it through all the verses of Dylan's, 'The Boxer.'

Mariah sang every Joni Mitchell song she knew a cappella, and the miles flew by into the night. Hours later, they were once again back in the civilization of the great metropolis of Houston, Texas.

CHAPTER 18 *Peter st. George*

"The Ranch is in danger, Hunter. I need to talk with you." Peter held his kitchen phone on his shoulder as he gazed out the window.

"OK. Is this a phone conversation?" Hunter asked in typical lawyer fashion.

"No, I think it's important that we meet in person, I'm not due in San Antonio for a couple of weeks. Are you in the mood for a getaway?"

"Sure, you sound serious. I can get away at lunchtime. That will put me in your area by mid afternoon. Sound good?"

"You're a good friend; glad I can count on you." Peter hung up.

Hunter arrived as promised. He was glad it was Indian summer, not as hot as July had been. He knocked on the screen door and walked on in. "OK, guy what's up?"

"I never told you this before—help yourself," Peter motioned to the fridge. Hunter grabbed a beer, "But you know I have strongholds here full of supplies. Just in case."

Hunter popped the cap off of his Corona. "Want one?"

"Sure. To get straight to the point, my sister's husband has been pressuring me to sell him my shares of the Ranch." Peter paused, to let that sink in. "I live here full time now. This is my home. It absolutely makes no sense." He rushed on, "He says I can stay on here, live here forever. The bottom line is, I don't trust him. My Mother gave me her shares of the Ranch before she died. Coupled with what I received from my grandfather, I have the controlling shares. I need to keep her trust, because I believe she had a reason."

After deciding to go to the Blue Spring, the two friends jumped in the jeep and bumped off over the stream. Hunter noted the glowing autumnal sycamores and pecan trees as Peter went on with his story. "You know, when Frank first threw out the idea casually at some holiday gathering, I just laughed and said, 'I live out there full time now; I didn't even know you knew the way.'"

The Texas air was cool and crisp. Neither spoke on the drive as the Jeep bumped through tall grass and rocky streambeds. Peter noticed things now others didn't. They heard a noise as they walked up to the deep pool of dark blue water. Peter saw a shy deer scurry away. They were there and they were watching. He had learned to recognize a presence in the silence. He wanted to completely confide in Hunter, but he was afraid he couldn't. He'd have to stick to legal issues. Hunter would question his sanity. The notions he had in his head were fanciful, unbelievable really.

Here I am, living out here all alone, Peter thought. He realized it had been at least a month since anyone had come out. That almost sounds crazy in itself. But Indians? Who would believe that? He had been calmly loving and nurturing the place for years now. But it had taken on new meaning when his suspicions began to take shape. At first it was just a shadow beneath the leaves of a tree. Then it was the sudden noises and the escaping deer. He had been staring into a dark cave once, then he thought his eyes were playing tricks on him; his clear blue eyes, that no longer squinted at the sun. He saw a face staring back at him.

Hunter had climbed the hill on the other side of the Blue Spring. He was now above the waterfall. He was exploring. A law degree and a flourishing practice hadn't stopped Hunter from becoming a Lad again once he was out here.

Peter resumed his reverie. He'd been looking into a dark cave. His eyes had gotten used to the dark. He suddenly realized that what he was looking at wasn't moving, or changing or going away. And it was human. A tall figure of a man, but not one he'd invited. He knew he was the only one out there. It was the middle of the week.

He looked up suddenly, Hunter was talking. "Hey, Pete, where did you go? I've been trying to get your attention for five minutes."

"I was just thinking. You know I'm a man of few words."

"What about?"

"Indians," he said the first thing that popped up.

"Indians? How long ago were the Indians out here?"

"The last sighting was in 1888; the Apache's attacked Lakeville."

"Are you coming across? I thought we'd walk upstream," Hunter suggested.

Peter joined Hunter. He wasn't sure how to start, so he decided to jump right in. "The Ranch is in danger. This land is not mine. I see myself as a steward. It is a big responsibility." The two were now following the creek draw above the cliff as they talked. "For the past three years life has been difficult out here. We are in a drought. I've been working on a large cistern on the high plateau to conserve rain water. It's far away from everything, no roads and no water. I spent all last summer putting in roads to reach deeper into the interior. It takes a lot of time and labor. This water tank is now complete and the animals will be able to get an adequate supply of water. There is no one in my family who even imagines or understands the work I'm doing out here. This is my life. It is my contribution to the universe. This has become my family, those I care for, those creatures I look out for."

"You mean all of the wildlife." Hunter looked up at his friend.

"Wild. Hmm? Who?" Peter said.

"Animals, Life. Are you OK? What you need is a good meal and someone to talk to."

"Yes, the land and what dwells here. This land belongs to them not to me. There are so few places left on earth in the natural habitat. I mean, society, most people enjoy society. People live with and are interdependent with one another. These left over expanses of land, the wilderness, must be allowed to just *be*. To exist unimpeded; not intruded upon. Maybe there is a God and he invented cities so that there would always be the country; a place where all Gods creatures could live on in safety. While Americans do and be and be done to in cities." Peter paused for breath.

He stopped. He who seldom spoke had spoken. He stopped walking. He stopped staring down at the dirt. He looked Hunter full on, straight into his pale blue eyes. "There are people in my family who insist on buying my shares of the Ranch. They will not take no for an answer. They are prepared to pay well. They would like me to continue my role as caretaker here. Frankly, I could use the funding for all these projects I mentioned."

Hunter stopped dead in his tracks. He stood quiet, his mind churning the implications. "Pete, they sound serious. What's up? You need to catch your breath and tell me all about it."

Peter continued, "I have protected The Ranch from grave diggers, from anthropologists, and other looters that would take her riches. My Grandfather even tested for oil back in the 40's. That proved unsuccessful, thankfully. Suddenly, the future of the oil business has many men desperate. I'm afraid to say my brother-in-law may be one of them."

Peter continued, "The ravaging of this precious earth, if they were to drill for oil here, is unpardonable. I'm at a complete loss of what to do. They have been hounding me for six months. At first I laughed, 'what would you want with The Ranch?' I asked. This place is a lot of work and a lot of responsibility. 'Oh, I have a plan,' he told me. 'I have elaborate plans.'

"My sister Ruby stayed out of it. She raises her family and does her social duties. She is actually out of touch with her husbands' business interests. I said, 'This is my life. I live here. Where would you have me go?' My grandfather gave me this land and this house and I promised him I would honor his gift." The two turned around and headed back towards the sound of the distant waterfall. "Actually, ever since George Bush got us involved in the Mid-East war, the global oil situation has intensified."

Hunter wanted to assure his friend, "You know, they have no legal right to do anything without your consent?"

Peter turned to Hunter and looked him straight in the eye. "I will defend this place with my life. The Life force that flows here now has been flowing here for over 2,000 years, slowly changing, but always here. On the other hand, Gilbert has been on this earth for about 60 years and hasn't learned a thing."

Hunter picked his words carefully. "I have known you for a lot of years Peter. You strike me as sort of Eastern in your mind-set about the world and possessions. You do not have the typical western material world view. In your consciousness about the earth, it seems you have become more so as you live here permanently."

Peter was thoughtful as they climbed down the narrow path, "Hunter, what if they are out here, spying, listening, and watching us?"

"Them who? Gilbert?" Hunter asked.

"No, I had forgotten about him for a moment. I was referring to the Indians, the forgotten tribe of Indians. You know, the ones that disappeared in 1888. What if they are still here?"

Hunter smiled, "Yes, I suppose they did live out here for a time. That explains why you find so many artifacts, arrowheads, and other signs. But really you know that was a long time ago. They would have died-out by now. Or if they are alive they'd be over a hundred years old. Face it, Geronimo was old when he turned himself in."

"Humor me for a moment. What if they kept the tribe alive, but hidden?"

"If that were the case, and I am sure it is not, you would know. You would have seen them, or heard them, or something," Hunter replied.

"Sometimes I get the feeling that I'm being watched. Does that ever happen to you when you are hiking alone?"

Hunter laughed, "Yes. I hear strange noises but it usually turns out to be one of the grandfather goats."

"Speaking of Indians, do you remember when Mariah spent the night in the tepee? I felt so aware of the Indians that night," Peter was tenacious.

"Peter, Mariah is not Indian she is French." Hunter thought he was taking this Indian thing too far. Was he losing it by being out here all the time by himself?

"Well you could have fooled me. Come to think of it, she seemed so calm and big eyed the next day. Like she wasn't so giggly and sparkley. Taking it all in."

"Perhaps she had some sort of Vision. Let's ask her." Hunter decided to go along with him.

"Seriously, Hunter," Peter smiled, "it is possible you know. I am not losing it. Don't look at me like that."

"We are behaving like ten-year-olds. If I were ten I would believe you. I guess I do feel like a teenager again when I'm out here. I will race you to the Blue Spring. First one there and in the water naked wins," Hunter laughed.

The two raced off. Soon they were at the cliffs edge, overlooking the blue spring below. Hunter hopped on the rocks on one foot while he struggled to pull off his shorts. Soon both were swimming in the crystal blue water. After some invigorating swimming and diving off the cliff. The two friends sat on the beach to let the sun dry them off.

"You know, funny you should mention her, but Mariah and her family camped out here just over a month ago," Peter said.

"Her family? Amazing, She already has a family?"

The sun lowered slowly in the west, and slipped behind a cliff. The leaves sparkled lime green on the pecan trees by the bank. "Hunter, do you mind driving the Jeep back to the house? I feel like walking," Peter asked, his somber mood returning.

"Sure, I will head back and get the grill going for some steaks."

"Thanks a bunch buddy." Peter half heard the familiar crunch of gravel as the jeep rolled over the stream and up the bank to the barely visible tire tracks.

Peter has the weight of the world on his shoulders, Hunter thought as he drove. But it was fun to imagine Indians out here. That lightened things up a bit.

Peter jammed his hands in his pockets and kicked around at the dirt. What was going on? Why in the world do they want his shares so badly? He saw something in the dirt and bent to pick it up. It was a very large, dusty, flint arrowhead. He smiled with a wistful tinge as he wiped it on his shorts and headed home.

CHAPTER 19 *Good Friday*

Every time it was a holiday, which translated meant a long weekend—David and Mariah endeavored to escape Houston. In keeping with their family tradition, they planned a trip to the Ranch. Mariah had views about family. Most of her traditions, she acquired from her own childhood. Like home cooked meals at home around the dining table, every night of the week—almost. Eating out was either a special occasion, or date night. And when homework and school activities got too intense, there was always Pizza night to fall back on. Family trips had always been her fondest memories, so she kept that tradition with her nuclear family. So instead of hanging with her siblings and their kids, like they did at Christmas, for Easter, David and Mariah planned a trip to the Ranch.

The only catch was, every time she'd called Peter, first to ask, then tell, of their plans to come, the phone rang and rang. They decided to go somewhere, anywhere as long as they were together, and out of town. With her usual faith, she kept calling and packing, and now, with the suburban fully loaded, they were barreling down the freeway.

"Did you call Peter, Mom?" asked Tristan.

"Yes, hon, I called him five times but he didn't answer. You know how big The Ranch is; he must be out on it somewhere."

Tristan was insistent.

Yet, Peter had to be there, didn't he? It was a huge place. Her timing with calling was just off.

Mariah marveled at Peter. She recalled again his friendly jovial manner—and his patience. Patience wasn't her virtue. And last time, there had been the disaster with the scorpion crawling in the wheel bed of the tire. It was a huge fierce creature. What an escapade. It had been over 100 degrees last summer. Now, it was early spring, and just pushing the high eighties. She craved everything about the Ranch. The energy of it pulled her through muggy Houston afternoons, and boring corporate meetings. She always dressed in office attire, usually black or navy suites, with her dark hair slicked tightly back. All the while, her heart beat with the rhythm of fresh pounding waterfalls, and her convictions were as stoic as white stone boulders, her being infused with the memory of their latest trips.

"We need to visit Peter. I promised I would be back," Tristan said.

"I haven't spoken to him, *yet*. We're all packed. We'll go to Austin first, camp there, try to reach him and go to The Ranch on Saturday. Of course, if we reach him, we can drive straight through to The Ranch."

Each mile brought them away from traffic congested freeways, to open shiny Texas roads, and winding hills over bridges of blue rivers. The four, equipped with all their camping gear, had been driving in silence, with David at the wheel. As they neared Austin, Mariah remembered Peter's serious face, and how he had given each one an arrowhead.

"Do you still have your arrowhead?" she asked Tristan.

"Of course, it's a treasure. Call Peter, Mom," urged Tristan again, shortly after they reached the Austin city limits.

"OK, OK, already." Bossy kids, Mariah thought.

They stopped for lunch at a vegetarian restaurant on Second Avenue. It was the typical Austin establishment. The place crawled with longhairs who ate beans, rice, and vegetables, and didn't believe in deodorant. They gathered at a table in the courtyard. Flies buzzed around the tables. The fresh tortillas looked good and the coffee smelled of spices.

"Mom, call him now," said Tristan.

Mariah sighed, "Okay, Okay." She rose from the table, and headed for the pay phone near the ladies room. She returned a few minutes later and shook her head.

"Still no answer. I guess we should go on to Pedernales State Park and set up camp for the night." She saw the look of disappointment cross Tristan's face. It mirrored her own.

A lot of people here reminded her of the days she spent in Summertown, Tennessee, with all the hippies from California who had gone there to start a commune. Long blonde hair, long beards, colorful tie-died clothing, and sandals. Isabella stared openly at one person's foot during lunch.

"His toes are hairy," she said wrinkling her nose. Mariah looked embarrassed and quickly ordered a carrot juice to keep from commenting.

They made the best of it, as they drove past Zilker Park and Barton Springs. The air smelled sticky and sweet like only spring in the Texas hill country could.

"It's too cool for air-conditioning and too hot in the sunshine without it," complained Mariah, as she alternated opening and closing her car window. "I feel itchy and sticky."

They were drinking ice-cold organic lemonade they had purchased from Whole Foods. Before long, they pulled into the Pedernales camp ground at dusk, fortunate to get the very last campsite.

Mariah played life by ear. That's why she would never have thought to call and reserve a campsite. She played piano by ear as well. Spontaneous; go where the spirit moved you, keep listening, keep paying attention. That was her motto. Now she had a whole family she was dragging around into the adventurous, spontaneous lifestyle. Sure, it would have been a disaster if they hadn't been able to snag the very last campsite, but they had, and now they were able to pitch their tents in the rosy glow of sunset.

"I'm used to summer camping where it stays light till nine. In spring we have less daylight. I forgot about that, sorry," she told David.

"We're on the lucky side of life," David responded.

"I hope we can go to The Ranch," Mariah said. "Bumper to bumper camping isn't really my thing. I cant believe we're sitting here listening to other people's radios play." She couldn't shake the feeling that they wouldn't get to The Ranch. Her thoughts played round and round in her head. What if Peter said no? The thought didn't make sense; Peter had never refused them. Still every time Tristan said, "You should call him. Why don't you call him? Call Peter, Mom," a thrill of dread went through Mariah. *'It heals us to go there.* David feels like a stranger to me lately. We're always bickering over silly little things. I'm sure it's all the financial stress now that I have started my own business. It's pure there, not tainted. It's very American pioneer. We feel safe and protected.' So her thoughts went.

Meanwhile Tristan kept on, "Call Peter, Mom."

In the leaden sky afternoon, they drug their lethargic bodies out of the hammocks where they had spent the morning engrossed in books. Mariah was reading William Styron's *Darkness Visible*. She had bought it for David incase he was depressed, or full of angst, or both, but he wasn't reading it. God knows it's tough being an artist. The Ranch will heal him. She was convinced of that, him, her, and *them*. Places were better than psychology books for healing. Case in point, in the very beginning, Styron listed how many creative people had committed suicide.

Regardless, they headed off on a long hike to the waterfalls. Isabella, now four, kept running ahead with Tristan, only to fall behind again when she was distracted by a butterfly or iguana. David and Mariah strolled along holding hands. They hiked along the ancient smooth stone riverbed, once molten lava, now eons later, solidified. It was a long smooth stroll to the waterfalls. The silver stream of water formed a channel within the wide riverbed. No one spoke, the water made enough noise. A strange dog joined them and ran alongside for a bit. Not a drop of sunshine to be found under this overcast, grey sky.

"I guess this is sort of a depressing day," Mariah said. "Kind of appropriate for Good Friday." A hawk flew over her head. She watched the bird for a long time.

"It's three o'clock," said David. "I'd like to stop and pray for a while."

They stopped beside a smooth grey stone. Mariah sat cross-legged as though meditating and prayed. David sat too. The kids kept exploring and playing with the dog. Tristan caught an iguana and showed it to people as they passed by. This far down the river was private. Mariah was very aware of the hawk. It seemed to be following her, as though to deliver a message. Considering what was about to happen, it made sense.

Mariah tilted her face up towards the sky. The tingle of raindrops was ever so light as it misted down. She opened her eyes. "It's misting a bit thick, and it's about to really rain, isn't it?"

They arose, untangled their crossed legs, gathered up the kids, and headed back to camp. All the while, the rain misting and stopping, and misting again. The rain fell hard just as they made it back to camp. All four squeezed into the tent, zipped it up and sat there, the rain pouring, thundering all around them.

"You know David, every time I come here, no matter what time of year, it does this."

"Let's call Peter," said Tristan again. "He has a house. We need to go there."

"OK," Mariah finally conceded.

Even as Mariah nodded to him, she realized she was scared to call. Just two days ago she'd sat with Kristen and Kate at Good Company Barbecue, reminiscing about all the good times they had at The Ranch. Like when Kristen had stolen the bottle of tequila and she and Kate had drank nearly the whole thing. Kristen had been a little imp back then, hiding out, throwing up in the bushes. They'd laughed about those days.

"OK, David. It's still pouring. Let's drive to the pay phone. What do we have to lose anyway?"

Mariah stood outside at the phone booth inthe rain. With cold fingers she jammed eighty cents into the slot. A voice answered, "Hello?"

"Hi, is Peter St. George there? This is Mariah Agnelli."

"Well no, not exactly." There was a pause.

"Hello. Hello?" Mariah asked.

"Uh, Peter cannot come to the phone now."

"Oh, I have been trying to call for several days with no luck..." A huge lightning flash and Mariah nearly dropped the phone. "Can you hear me?"

Another pause before the voice on the line said, "Peter is no longer with us."

"Huh?" It took a few moments for it to sink in, and then begin spreading through her veins like ice water. "What happened?"

"Peter has been brutally murdered." Click. The phone went dead.

Mariah stumbled through the torrential downpour to the car in shock. "Peter's dead," she announced in a flat voice. She stood there frozen, the rain flooding her vision. Then she jumped quickly into the front seat. The rain now mixed with hail still pelted the car. Hair dripping, her face streaming with water, she said, "My dream! I dreamed this. Over a year ago, I dreamed that Peter died. I can't believe this." She pushed at the water streaming down her face as she explained to David, still struggling with the reality. "It was at Easter time."

David pulled more quarters from his pocket and handed them to Mariah. "It *is* Easter time."

With shaking hands she went to feed the phone again. "Hi, I'm Mariah from Houston," she calmed herself with slow breaths,

"Steven French's daughter. I've known Peter for years."

"Hey, Mariah, I'm Michael, I used to work out here on The Ranch. I'm also a close friend of Peter's. They called me to come out here from where I've been working with the Peace Corp. You wouldn't want to come here now. The sheriff's here. The family's here. The police are all over the place." He paused. "It's a crime scene."

The story he told was cold and brutal. "There were three teens, driving an old Ford farm truck. When Peter greeted them at the door in front of his house, the boys took out the gun. The tallest boy hoisted the shotgun up on his shoulder, took aim, and fired. That's the version I heard by the time it trickled through the grapevine. The boys then panicked and took off without taking anything." After a pause he explained. "The youngest one, only seventeen, vomited when he got home. He broke down and told his mother. They notified the sheriff, and he came out and found Peter's body already cold stone dead. As a result of this one teen's confession, he was only seventeen; all three boys were taken into custody. Cold-blooded murder, it seems. The sheriff and a team are out here investigating everything."

Michael's voice broke, "I don't know how to say this, but Peter had been dead for twenty-four hours before anyone found him. He was shot at close range. They shot him straight in the face at close range."

Mariah couldn't speak as shock and grief filled her.

"And they found bullets in his back too. They shot him three times. I'm not from here. But everybody knows everyone. It's very weird. These are local high school kids for Christ's sake. It makes no sense. I'm heartbroken. Peter's families livid. You can imagine."

"I am sorry," Mariah said." Thanks for telling me what happened."

She hung up. She turned to see David and her two little ones beside the car covered in a rain grey mist in the dimming light, the sky having spent its rage.

Mariah didn't want to discuss the gruesome details in front of

131

the kids. "Peter has died," she said bluntly. That was all they needed to know.

"Can we still go?" Tristan was still urgent.

"Well, no. His friend Michael said there is a whole big mess over there." She could just imagine; the stench of death, his family, the neighbors. The investigators trooping around examining everything.

"But we want to see Peter. We want to go to The Ranch," Tristan argued.

Mariah put her arms around them. Not today honeys. The bedraggled group held each other in the drizzle, too shocked to move.

Later, when they had a good blaze going to help dry the dampness of their water logged campsite, Mariah tucked her kids into their sleeping bags. Both of the tents were soaked. Alone with David beside the fire, Mariah broke the tense silence. "I'll tell you what I managed to piece together so far, but what's weird is my dream. It flashed on me just as Michael told me the news."

"Michael said that Peter was left alone, lying on the ground, dead. In contrast, let me tell you my dream." Mariah went on to read to David the dream she had written down over a year ago in her journal.

"I dreamed that I was at The Ranch. *It was late in a grey afternoon. I was sitting in a grassy meadow, in a large circle, with a group of Indian elders. There was a fire in the center, even though it was daylight. Peter wasn't with us. I questioned the leader, a stocky muscular guy with grey hair cut short. His features were Indian, his skin swarthy. In answer to my question he pointed up. He said, "Peter has left this earth." I thought, 'what?' He pointed up in the direction of the smoke. I saw Peter, his arms outstretched like Jesus as he rose up to the sky with the smoke. I saw white bilious clouds parting with a huge orange sun shining through. It was like seeing a vision. "He is no longer here, but we have a Gift he entrusted us to give you."*

"But who are you?" I interjected.

"We are the elders of this Land." He gestured expansively with a deliberate reach of his muscular arms. "The gift is why we are all gathered here. We have decided you are to inherit this land."

"Me? But I am not family. I live in Houston. I only come out here three or so times a year." I looked at the serious faces of the elders gathered around. This was a serious gift. I must accept." Mariah looked up at David as she finished.

"As I watched Peter float up, it made me feel that quiet, patient, unassuming, generous Peter was somehow going to be all right. His death was not a tragedy, but something sacred. Or his life was sacred and he should be honored in death."

David watched Mariah as she spoke. Half her face glowed red in the firelight framed by the black darkness surrounding them.

"David, that dream was a year and a half ago. I thought it was symbolic. Peter rising up like that made me think of Jesus in His Ascension to Heaven. I didn't know humans could do that. But now Peter at age thirty-five is dead. Snatched from life in his prime. And tonight is Good Friday. It's like Easter in real life. I really want to go to The Ranch now. Perhaps I did inherit something." She looked around at the darkness that enveloped them, "But I feel frightened. Suddenly this darkness that surrounds us is no longer a cool velvet black sky. Instead it's thick, heavy and oppressive. Ink black. A starless blanket concealing evil as it lurks just beneath the surface. A senseless killing, as if God is not in his Heaven and evil is loosed on the earth."

David reached out and touched her knee. He could tell the romance he'd anticipated for this trip was on hold. The two lay next to each other on separate sleeping bags, each cocooned in their aloneness. After a restless night, they awoke to a gloomy sunless morning. The air was chilled. The trees still dripped water from the flood of rain the day before. The chores of camping felt tedious now.

"Kids, we'll hike back to the river in a bit. But I've got to get this breakfast cleaned up," Mariah yelled.

"Can we play Frisbee in the meadow while you get ready?" Tristan asked, stunned by her tone.

"Fine." Mariah slapped a fat mosquito. The blood burst on her arm. "I hope we can find out more details soon. I wonder if they'll have a memorial service?" she asked David.

"It doesn't make any sense," David replied. "It's not logical. Peter's out there with tons of possessions, guns, jeeps, boats, food, whiskey, and cash too. He has prized movie cameras and stereos. So they just murder him and leave?"

"It doesn't make sense," Mariah repeated. "He's very wealthy. My dad always hinted at that. But he never talked specifics. I do know he didn't work; he lived on his trust fund."

"I'll tell you what. Let's break camp early. We can go into Austin and all have a big swim at Barton Springs. The fun's kind of gone out of this."

The trees are in mourning Mariah thought. It was Holy Saturday now and the light had gone out of the world for real now. Not just symbolically.

"The fun has gone out for Peter, that's for sure. To think we have been talking about him all week and he was already dead. You know I called before we left. The phone just rang, and rang, and rang in his house. It might have just happened and no one had found him yet." Mariah shook herself. "I feel selfish. I hate that one of the good ones was murdered, but I also hate this feeling of evil that pervades nature now."

David opened his arms wide and Mariah buried her face in his chest. She cried then. Then he held her. Where was the motive? Since the youngest teen had lost his nerve--run straight home and told his mom--the body was discovered sooner rather than later. Twenty-four hours after the execution is a long time. Why had the teens fled without stealing anything? As the boy had confessed, there was no need for an investigation. "Thrill Killing" is how the local paper described it. "Teen suicide, teen runaway, and now we have teen murderers. What's wrong with this picture?"

Mariah and David went back to their campsite. The light had gone out. The earth was indeed a cold and lonely place. The rain stopped. The sun finally came out strong and dried everything, but the sun had never seemed so harsh to Mariah. Darkness Visible lay tossed in the tent where she'd thrown it. She shivered in the bleak April day, Holy Saturday, the day before Easter, and the light had gone out. She could relate.

"Oh no, we can never go back to The Ranch," she wailed. "It was the Garden of Eden. It was purity made manifest. No fear there. I trusted every person, every animal I saw. Peter was like St. Francis of Assisi; he was happy, and helped the wild animals."

But young Tristan wondered about the Indians. He was sure he'd seen an Indian the last time he'd been there. Oh why had he given the fish back? Who would believe him? How can he ever go back?

Mariah kept replaying her dream in her mind. *The Indian elders of the Land, the rightful owners, had a gift. They wanted to present her with a gift.* How would she ever be able to return? She had known no one really except for Peter. He was her one contact with that amazing Texas wilderness. The gate to paradise had slammed shut. Regardless, when she closed her eyes each night for many years after, she could see that vision of a man, his arms outstretched, rising up into wondrous stormy sun-filled clouds, and on into the heavens.

CHAPTER 20 *Hunter*

Mariah settled in on her brilliant deck with a strong cup of coffee, when her solitude was interrupted by a ring. She dove for the phone.

"Mariah?" The voice on the other end of the line inquired.

"Yes, who is this?"

"Hunter."

She paused, as the voice from the past speeded in to her present. She groped for the chair and sat down, propping her tan legs on the table. "You got my message?"

"Yes, I thought about what you said about Peter. I think we should meet. Can you come to San Antonio?"

"Name the time and place." After some good natured banter, Mariah hung up, contemplating the significance of seeing Hunter again. It had been a few years.

She strode across the crowded café, her cowboy boots clopping on the tile floor, and then she spotted Hunter at a two top by the window. His reddish blond hair glinted in the sunlight, his eyes squinting behind wire frames. Suited up like any other lawyer, she'd have spotted him anywhere, even after all the years. His clean white shirt buttoned up the seriously individual interior.

Mariah flashed back to their first meeting. It was at that famous Schoolhouse trip. She remembered everyone had taken charge and prepared a feast. Mariah had quickly gotten acquainted with Hunter. As she'd listened to him she found him fascinating, it was as if they were two introverts who found each other. Although he was an advanced law student he was fun, not a snob. He was a committed outdoors man. Here in Texas everyone she met had a love for the land. The thought of Peter, put a fresh pang in her heart. He was the sole reason she was here.

Hunter beamed at the big smile that had gotten Mariah the nickname *Sunshine* in college. They hugged.

"I know your time is tight, but it is wise to meet in person." Mariah did not waste time on small talk. "I don't believe Peter's death can be easily explained away," Mariah launched in. "Did they even investigate?"

"Whoa, slow down." Hunters smile froze. He offered her a seat.

"Being from Houston, my visits have been mostly annual, but I had known him for over fifteen years. I have been going to The Ranch since I was sixteen. I don't know any of his friends. I know the memorial service was private with a closed casket because of the damage to his body. I'm a complete outsider. But you were his best friend."

The waitress appeared, interrupting her monologue.

"I'd like a Greek salad with chicken," Mariah smiled without taking a breath. She had been leaping from point to point and wasn't sure if she had lost Hunter along the way.

"I'd like the same with a side of hummus and pita," Hunter spoke slowly enunciating each word to the young waitress who'd come to take their order. "You're talking about motive, I presume."

"I'm talking about the lack of investigation. Once someone confesses there's no need for further exploration. Yes, the questions of motive, or who benefits from Peter's death, were never asked."

"I think you're partly right." Hunter tilted slightly forward. "About six months before the shooting, Peter called me. I met him out there, Mariah. He wouldn't talk on the phone. At the time I thought the heat and the isolation were taking a toll on him mentally. I moved my schedule around and took some weekdays off. He wanted a private meeting. I thought I could catch up on some paperwork so I agreed to run out. It was just the two of us. Peter was acting strange. He wouldn't talk in the house. We had decided to go out to the Blue Spring for a hike."

"And?" Mariah invited.

Hunter relayed the events. "Peter was quite upset. He went on and on about the importance of his life there. He actually said, *'This has become a way of life for me. It is my contribution to the universe. I have a sense of family with those I care for. Those creatures I look out for.'* His main concern was that his Brother-in-law wanted to buy his shares of the land."

"I can see why that would upset him," Mariah said.

"He was so concerned. I understand about wildlife, but he was talking crazy. Then he said, his Ranch was *'A place where all Gods creatures could live on in safety.'*"

"That sounds wise. Unbelievable, true. St. Francis cared more for animals than humans. Its a gift really to be so in tune with nature." Mariah was a bit stunned at the revelation.

We met last fall. I swear he thought there were Indians out there on the Ranch. I tell you. I have been coming out there for years. I've been all over and never seen anything.

By the time Hunter had finished his story Mariah was scraping hummus and the last piece of feta on the pita bread. Her green eyes were wide with suspended belief. "God, that's weird." A chill crept over her as she contemplated the implications. "Well, that could mean that my suspicions are more than just suspicions."

"The list of random crazy killings is well known. Let's walk." Hunter rose, paid the check and stood by her chair as she gathered her jacket and purse, and scrambled up. The door shut on the noisy restaurant as they emerged into the tree-lined street. "We can walk to my office from here." He continued, "The list—Kennedy, Martin Luther King, John Lennon—all shot by a crazy killer. When famous people are shot in broad daylight, there's little investigation because the crazy killer has witnesses."

"It's one year since Peter's death and what's happening?"

"The three boys are locked up. They have different sentences based on age, which one pulled the trigger, and..."

"...And the witness?" Mariah interrupted, "The third one, the boy who held the flashlight for the other two?"

"He confessed ... or told on his friends," Hunter said. "He claimed ignorance of their plan."

"He confessed?"

"He came forward right away. He told on his buddies. He wasn't confessing, so much as going to the police with the story. Like a witness to horrible crime. After he reported it, the Sheriff drove on out to Peter's Ranch. By the time the Sheriff found Peter, he'd been dead for 24 hours. The boy had no idea he was under suspicion, and later, after extensive isolation and interrogation, he was sentenced and convicted.

"Afterwards, under duress, the killers confessed to the murder," Hunter explained.

"Killing in the middle of nowhere. It wouldn't have worked if there wasn't a witness," Mariah said.

"The witness was fully compliant. He gave a full description of the other boys and what had transpired at the murder," Hunter said. "The cops were able to apprehend the other two boys from their classrooms at the local High School.

"They were back in class the day after committing murder?" Mariah asked.

"The witness claimed the teen, Jared, 17, shot Peter in cold blood," Hunter said. "Shot him point blank in the face with a shotgun. He apparently thought it was funny.

"The witness claimed innocence, and complete ignorance of their plan. His friends allegedly invited him to drive them out to find summer jobs. They let him in on it, in exchange for a ride. Neither boy had a car. The court charged him as an accessory because he drove the vehicle. Peter would still be alive if he hadn't driven the killers to the Ranch. They all got short sentences because they were tried as juvies."

"It's not fair. It's not justice. But I do not believe it anyway. Was there an investigation? Motive? Other suspects, or anything?" Mariah asked.

"Well, no," Hunter said. "The crime scene became contaminated immediately. And once the Sheriff had his killer's sworn confession; case closed."

"No further investigation?" Mariah asked.

"No. The family wanted it settled as quickly as possible," Hunter said. "Less publicity, you know."

"Uh, huh. It's fishy, not right," Mariah said. "Not Justice for Peter."

"Well," Hunter said, "Peter is gone. No matter how long you debate the how and the why."

"True, true. God I miss him," Mariah said.

Hunter liked to seem open-minded. "You think it was planned, masterminded?"

"You cannot tell me, that a man with the controlling shares of nineteen thousand acres out here in the middle of West Texas, is randomly killed for no reason?"

"As the driver, Kenny was sentenced with manslaughter," Hunter said. "In juvenile court no less. It's true, it was a rather short sentence."

"Peter wasn't even robbed for chrissake. And no one is asking questions?" Mariah tapped her boot and fumed unsatisfied. Was he deliberately evading her?

"Look, I know, but there are a lot of millionaires in Texas." Hunter was diplomatic. "They are an important family, the sheriff had to close the case quickly. No one wants that kind of publicity."

"You're right, the Kings, King Ranch, the Bushes..." The list went on for days. "And there are a lot of loners living alone in the middle of nowhere," she added, "only they are still alive."

"You know I can't have this conversation, especially in broad daylight." Hunter was backing out, she noticed. Mariah jumped up on a low wall beside the sidewalk and strode. She should change the subject.

"Cool boots," he said.

"Yay, I'm a Texan," she said.

"Don't you ever grow up?"

"I hope not," Mariah grinned.

"Look, I have kids. I have one foot in the real world, and two feet in fairyland here; the math doesn't make sense."

"No, and Peter's brutal murder doesn't either," Mariah shrugged. She knew she shouldn't push it.

There was a long pause before Hunter spoke. He stopped and turned towards her. "It was a gay killing."

Mariah had heard everything now. "Peter was not gay."

"You and I know that. But he was an eccentric, living out there, hiring workers to build the roads and water cisterns to catch rainwater for the *wild life*."

Mariah turned and faced him, her hands on her hips. "It was a twelve year drought."

"For deer," he concluded.

The two walked in silence, both contemplating, side by side. "Look Mariah-girl, I'm a lawyer, my father was a lawyer, and my grandfather was a lawyer. Career, family, societal obligations..." Hunter back-peddled fast.

"Sweet."

"Yeah, Peter was my friend. I loved him. I'll never go back out there." Hunter looked down and shook his head.

"All right. How's his family doing?" Mariah tried a new tack.

"Well, his sister died at Thanksgiving."

Mariah raised an eyebrow.

"Of food poisoning," he clarified.

"I see." She didn't see.

"Not connected," he explained.

"Of course not." But Mariah thought something was out of place.

"The Ranch will forever be a beautiful memory for me. I feel like

141

I grew up there." He stopped and faced her. "It was really good to see you." He stuck his hand out formally.

"You too," Mariah looked past his wire framed glasses to those pale watery eyes. "Later." She didn't take the offered hand, she saluted, then turned and headed towards the busy street and the shops.

CHAPTER 21 *Wilderness*

"I have a surprise for you," David announced as he entered the house.

Mariah was in the kitchen preparing broccoli and squash for the steamed veggies they usually had for summer dinners. He walked up behind her and put his strong arms around her. She leaned into the embrace a minute before turning her face towards him.

"Shall I guess?"

"Impossible. As you already know, my parents are taking Tristan and Isabella to Florida for a Disney vacation."

"They're thrilled." She added onions and mushrooms to the mix.

"I thought we could take a trip of our own while they're gone."

"Yeah?" This could be interesting, she thought.

"A camping trip to West Texas. I thought we could camp at the KOA campground in one of those small Texas towns and then take a day hike to The Ranch from there. Just to check it out. See what's happening to the place these days."

For once Mariah didn't interrupt, just stared up at him in astonishment. It was perfect. He was on a roll. She was speechless. Over dinner they made their plans. After supper they continued talking as they had their evening stroll through their neighborhood. Next to them, Isabella rode her tricycle while Tristan rode his bike twenty feet ahead, then looped back.

They already had most of the gear they needed, but David thought a new tent would be nice as an anniversary present.

"Ten years of marriage," he said when he lugged the big, hastily wrapped gift into the house. "You having fun yet?"

"I think it's about to get really good. Seven days without kids. What will we ever do with ourselves?"

"I don't know what to expect. We could just take daypacks with all the supplies."

At the last minute, David's parents had to cancel the Florida trip. "I'm sorry, Mariah." David looked really bummed.

"You know, I'm not. We'll just take the kids. They love The Ranch too, and they're older now - they'll be able to appreciate it more." She smiled. "Especially Isabella—she was so young when we were last there. Come to think of it, I actually hate for them to miss it."

"That's my girl." David grabbed her hand as they went to break the news to the kids. "I know you're disappointed about the Florida trip being put on hold, but it's just a postponement. Your grandparents will take you next month. In the meantime, how would you like another Hill Country Texas camping trip?"

Tristan and Isabella looked up from the chess game they were playing. Their solemn faces morphed into happy ones as their eyes grew wide in the dawn of understanding.

* * *

They found the familiar turn-off from the highway. And now they were on the drive through the tunnel of live oaks. "My dad will kill me if he finds out I trespassed." Mariah was nervous about this new idea of just driving in as if nothing had happened.

"Well, how did Matt Weston find The Ranch in the first place? We're just exploring." David patted her knee.

* * *

Mariah heard her children's voices in the distance. Now they had trespassed. With a few daypacks they had made the trek to Indian point and set up for the day. She had decided to stay and swim in Jade Cove. She stared into the blue sky, as she floated on the double air mattress she had been relaxing on, and had now floated to the middle of Jade Cove. She must have drifted off. She looked around with a start, she was far from shore and everyone was gone. Without warning, Isabella, Tristan, and David suddenly rose up from under water and dumped her in. Surprise attack. She fell shocked, and thankful, from the scorching heat into the cold water. She played dead instead of reacting to the attack, and kept sinking deeper under water. She slipped into the green silent depths holding her breath as long as she could before rushing up to the surface for air. As she floated down she took in her surroundings. It was a whole new world down here. This definitely deserves exploring she thought. She burst from the silent depths into screams and shouts.

"Mom, we thought you were drowning. You scared us. What a strange reaction." She swam over to retrieve the air mattress. She held onto it, but stayed immersed in the water. "Where have you been all day?" they asked in unison.

"Just here. What time is it? Are you guys ready for lunch?" Mariah asked. She lazily trailed her fingers in the water as she watched Tristan and Isabella clamor up the rock bank back at shore. "Where have you been all day anyway?"

"We've been at the schoolhouse." The children spoke in unison.

"I lost all track of time guys. What can I say?" Mariah smiled at Tristan. "How was the trip to the schoolhouse?"

"You won't believe this."

"Try me."

"Well, when we went to the schoolhouse, there were some steps leading down from a door in the floor."

"Door in the floor?" she repeated.

"Yeah. We thought it was a hidden basement or something, but it led to a tunnel."

Mariah's eyebrows rose. "And?"

"We went through. It opened up to a large room, like a cellar, it was lined with shelves, and full of supplies. Canned food and all sorts of stuff."

Mariah looked at David. "Were you with them?"

He gave a look as if to say, of course. "Tristan's, right. There was a complete stronghold of supplies, hidden under the schoolhouse."

"Perhaps Peter was planning for something. Lots of people do these days. Trying to be prepared. You know, just in case." Mariah speculated.

"In case of what?" David asked.

"In case the world ends in 2021, or perhaps an alien invasion," Mariah said.

"Mom, one day in the sun and you have lost it." Tristan shook his head.

"He had to have some reason for putting those things there. Hmm, I wonder what he was thinking. Seems curious doesn't it?" Mariah said.

Tristan shrugged. "Well, we didn't touch anything. But it's cool to know if we come out here again this place is stocked up," he said.

"Seems Peter was in the process of stocking it," David added. "The shelves weren't all full, but it doesn't seem as though anyone else has been down there. Nothing has been touched."

Mariah looked at the faces of her two children. "Any other secrets to share?"

Their faces grew serious and repentant, "Mom, we need to tell you something."

They looked so cute and worried. Mariah wondered what on earth could be the matter. "OK. I'm all ears. Shoot."

"We suspect there are still Indians out here." Tristan was as serious as she had ever seen him.

Mariah's eyes widened. "Oh? "Explain yourselves. Did you see any?"

"Well, yes and no. But who else were all those supplies for?"

Mariah shrugged. "Like I said, alien invasion?" She paused, "What did you mean by yes and no?"

"Well, I did sort of, not today, though. I saw him when we were here before." He shook his head. "I always thought we'd have a chance to explore later—with Peter." I had no idea this could happen! That Peter could die and we'd never come again and we'd never be able to ask him, directly," Tristan said.

"I know," Mariah said, "But now we're back, and you can still go looking for the Indians." She'd always done this with her children—went along with the fantasy. It made them feel comfortable telling her things—although Tristan was getting a little old for fantasy.

"We haven't seen them now. They could have gone into hiding. Anyway, we'd like to take a little hike, is that OK?"

"Now? It's already after four." Was this a new game Tristan was playing with Isabella? "Oh, all right, which direction?" Sounds fun she thought, I hope they find some. She swung her legs back over the air mattress to resume her floating.

"Over there. We'll look for firewood when we get back. Thanks. Mom." He turned to Isabella. "You do want to come, don't you? You can handle it?"

"Of course." Isabella rolled her eyes. "I can handle it."

"Not too far. We will have dinner eventually. We'll have a nice fire with the wood you gather. Remember it's a little cold at night." She glanced at David who was still smiling.

Isabella got down on one knee to tie her laces. Her hair was long down her back with bangs pulled out of her face. She seemed older than her six years. With her eyes on her brother, she pulled the knots tight and chased after him.

Tristan spoke confidingly, "I think we should explore the cave we were in with Peter." Mariah heard Tristan say this as she watched them tromp down the path. Her heart tugged as she watched the brave souls. They would be fine. They were the only ones out here for miles. If she acted clingy they would never be so strong. The world in the city had become full of arranged outings and play dates. This freedom was refreshing for everyone.

Later they were all back at the makeshift camp. Mariah saw Tristan's look of quiet discouragement, and Isabella's exhilarated, dirty face. Mariah shook her head at her daughter's grass stained knees. She's such a climber.

"Hi kids, how about a hug?" Mariah, now changed from her swim and dry, her hands full, bent for a kiss and a one-armed hug. "How are my troopers? Did you find some Indians out there?"

"Good," Tristan kicked the dirt. "No. I wish Peter was here. I can't believe this. All this time I couldn't really believe what happened to him. What's going to happen now?"

Mariah avoided the unpleasant question. "Would you guys like some supper? I have some turkey sandwiches here. Wait, have you guys seen your dad? It's getting late and he's not one to miss his meals."

"No, I haven't."

"Wow. I thought he'd caught up with you guys. Come on over, we'll have a little picnic." Mariah glanced around as they situated themselves at the old picnic table. She had a platter of sliced salami and cheese, crackers, and apples along with the sandwiches. "Isabella, don't we have some Fritos somewhere?"

Isabella dug in the backpack and pulled out an open bag of Fritos. Usually they'd come out here with a car full of stuff; tents, cook stove, campfire. The tables were still here, and the latrine in the woods. Everything seemed just as they'd seen it two and a half years ago. They heard a noise in the distance. They jerked to attention, but all was still.

"I keep hearing noises. It's different now. I'm worried that someone will catch us. Or us them," Mariah said.

"Daddy, Daddy!" Isabella pointed in the distance.

"What's he doing over there?" Mariah muttered as she chewed. David walked up to his family, the only people for miles in every direction.

"I have a concept ..." David began as he fished for a beer in the cooler, "...tomorrow, bright and early, we should plan a hike to the Blue Spring. I know it's far, but we may never get to come here again. We should start early and spend the day." He pulled out the beer and popped it open. "We should make the most of what is probably our last trip."

"Can I jump off the cliff?" Tristan was excited.

Mariah nodded, "Good idea. Of course you can." Then she looked at David, "Sounds wonderful, Honey. Help yourself." She gestured to the sandwich spread. David took a swig and scooted in. They discussed the plans for the next day's adventure. Mariah was happy to avoid the gruesome thoughts of Peter and how he died. The brutal fact of murder was incongruous with the beauty and peace of the place.

CHAPTER 22 *Blue Spring*

The family embarked on the three-mile hike in the quiet morning. After a few miles, salty sweat dripped into Mariah's eyes. She heard the water loud in the distance as they neared the Blue Spring. She watched the trail for signs of life and was rewarded with the sight of deer prints in the soft earth. She followed them dreamily, and then stopped abruptly when she noticed footprints next to them. They looked like they had been made by moccasins.

"Wait." She turned around to see the deer prints again, but they were covered with her own footprints now. She hoped no one was out here. Really they were trespassing—but they meant no harm.

"Mom. Mom!" Tristan was talking to her.

"Yes? Did you say *hiding*?" Mariah asked.

"Peter said if they were found out, they may go into hiding."

"They? Who?"

"The Indians," he hissed.

"Did he actually say there were Indians here?"

"No, not exactly...I just thought so. I told him what I had seen and he just said to be careful."

"You never told me that before, Tristan. And it's been over two years since you've seen Peter or been here."

Tristan shrugged, "Well I am telling you now because if they are here I want to find them."

Mariah thought for a moment about the footprints. She remembered shape-shifting. Indians know how to do that. "Tristan, do you remember seeing any deer since we got here?"

"Yes, we've seen several. Four or five, alone, at different parts of the terrain. They seem to appear from nowhere."

"Yes, and run away. That's been my experience," Mariah said.

"Well of course they do. There aren't any people here. It's not like the Smoky Mountains, where deer are used to humans," David said.

When they rounded the bend Isabella squealed, "We're here!" There was the waterfall at Blue Spring. "It looks smaller than I remember it."

"That's because you are so big now." Mariah hugged Isabella with one arm as they walked side by side.

"Last one in is a screaming Banshee!" shouted Tristan. He threw off his T-shirt and dove right in. He screamed, "It's cold!"

"How are we going to climb the waterfalls without a rope?" Mariah asked.

"We'll figure it out," David assured her. That was the least of their worries. "Here we are—one last swim. Let's just enjoy the peace of this perfect day." David jumped in next, then Isabella. Mariah had on her new black swimsuit and the sun felt really nice on her skin. Swimming here wasn't the lazy cool of Jade Cove. This spring was pure ice.

"Get in Mom," they all yelled at her. Mariah stood, her feet numbing out in the icy water. She watched the crystal water climb up her legs, as she inched her way in. She shivered in the bright sun, chill bumps on her arms and torso.

"Look at me!" Shouted Tristan.

Mariah looked up. David and her son were already at the cliff top, their brown bodies silhouetted against the sun. What handsome young ones, she thought. David did a graceful swan dive off the edge. Look at him fly, thought Mariah. He's so physical, he's always graceful. One minute poised on the top of the cliff like a Greek statue, one leg bent, hands by his sides. Some people are awkward in their nudity, but not him. And now he dives as though flying through the air. Smooth as a bird. Out here he's different, she mused. He's relaxed, he flows, and he has tons of energy. Creative ideas just

flow out of him. She remembered the anxiety of their city life. The almost constant scowl that disfigured his handsome features, his shoulders rose almost to his ears in tension as he bickered over little things; the inevitable bills and stressors of life. Even yelling at her for doing an oil painting instead of cleaning the bathroom. Here there were no bathrooms to clean. It was hard to picture now. He was scrambling up a waterfall, glancing over his shoulder, a big grin lit up his whole face. This spring must be the fountain of youth, she mused.

He looked at her with no strings attached, no hidden agendas. As if he were just happy to be alive, happy to be here. She was only waist deep in water and totally numb. She dove in and swam under water into the mysterious blue-green depths with waving palm fronds. It was over thirty feet deep she'd been told. On the surface, she spread her arms like wings as she swam a slow circle, swimming hard toward the force of the waterfall she relaxed her body to let the water push her away. Suddenly David was beside her, his strong arm encircled her while she swam with the other one. She turned on her back and floated.

"I'm afraid if I stop swimming I'll freeze," her teeth chattered.

"You're beautiful," he said.

"I am?" she asked, taken by surprise. Yes, she was beautiful, and she knew that, as she floated in the coolness of the spring. "Where are the kids?"

"Over the cliff. Tristan is going to jump in a minute, but he's playing it cautious."

"Yes, that's his way," she mused. Tristan appeared at the top of the cliff.

"We're watching," she shouted.

"Here goes." Tristan jumped, his small body made a huge splash from the fifteen foot height. Tristan emerged for air, then dove back under.

Mariah ducked under to see how far she could see under water. Tristan was down far. He's an underwater guy, Mariah thought of her son. She came back up gasping for air. She watched the water for signs of his return. Still he hadn't surfaced. She kicked hard again, trying to see in the blue underwater.

CHAPTER 23 *Water*

"David! Tristan is still underwater!" Mariah choked as she shouted above the pounding water fall.

They both darted back in and began to swim deeper. Tristan was somewhere down there swimming hard as if he was trying to reach the bottom. Mariah came up for air. Was David going deeper? Isabella, she thought, where was she?

"Isabella, can you hear me?" The waterfall crashed. They were in the middle of nowhere and no one knew they were here. "Isabella!" Mariah gulped water as she shouted.

She pulled herself up the waterfall. Her fingers dug into the crevices. Her heart beat fast. Finally she was up, on the boulders beside the stream. She prayed to God, a hurried prayer under her breath. Here she was, she thought guiltily, enjoying a romantic moment with her true love—that happened to be her husband. She had taken her attention from her beloved children and put them in danger. She'd never forgive herself if anything happened.

In the pool, Tristan sank fast. He loved to swim underwater, but this was something new. Something like seaweed was stuck to his ankle; he closed his eyes and held his breath. The water rushed towards him. His nose and ears hurt. The colors were beautiful. There were all kinds of green and bluish-green ferns under water. Coral colored, black and white fish, even pink and blue fish. All sizes. They must laugh when I fish, he thought. As he studied his surroundings he noticed a large gold-orange fish shimmered just ahead. He followed it to get a better look. It had disappeared

under a jutting rock into the depths. It shimmered with quicksilver luminescence. He pulled himself through and was surprised to see a tunnel through the stone. He kicked hard through the tunnel and followed a light in the distance. Curiosity fueled him. The tunnel narrowed to darkness and he almost panicked. Then he saw a silver shimmer of fish glistening ahead. He hoped for an outlet. Then he squeezed through.

His mind blanked for a moment and then cleared. He saw a dim greenish light far away. He was still underwater, yet he was breathing. His fear replaced by the majesty of it all. He was neither hot nor cold. It was dim, but his eyes grew accustomed to the surreal glow. This was definitely a cave. A cave full of crystals he soon realized. It was similar to the crystals they had found before, but many more shapes and colors. He felt like he had landed within a treasure. Somehow the whole discovery, being in such a hidden place was a treasure in itself.

He looked about him. Gradually dim shadowy shapes took form in the cave. Before him a young man sat cross-legged, his long black hair flowed around him like a mantle. He beamed a huge white smile at Tristan. The Indian picked up Tristan's hand and studied his palm. Then he touched it slowly with long brown fingers. As he closed Tristan's hand around a stone he looked into his eyes. He nodded for Tristan to open his hand. When Tristan obeyed, a butterfly flashed its colorful wings, as it flew about the cave. Tristan's green eyes brightened as he watched. It was the same kind of butterfly he and Isabella had seen before—their last trip here. Was this the same Indian, the one who had caught the fish for him a few years earlier? The Indian laughed at his gift. Tristan wore a small gold cross around his neck. He fingered it as he wondered if he needed to give something. He realized he clutched something in his other hand. He had grabbed it on the way down.

The rock was hard on his palm. He offered the stone to the Indian, but as he opened it the stone changed, it began to sparkle like a diamond. It rapidly melted and became a pool of silver liquid and then dark like blood. Tristan thought the Indian had worked more magic on him, but the Indian was amazed by the apparent magical powers of Tristan. He offered a bowl and they poured the handful of blood in the bowl. Tristan's memory sparked, he remembered something sad and distant and far away. A maiden near him bowed her head. He looked at her crown of blue-black hair, the glossy sheen fairly floating above her head. She raised her head and seemed young and fresh, yet solemn. She backed away.

"You have brought me here." Tristan acknowledged of his present situation. The Indian nodded and smiled.

"I have been searching for you," said Tristan. "Since I thought I imagined you on the bank, with the fish."

He nodded.

"What is your name? Do you speak English?" The words tumbled out before Tristan, realized he was doing all the talking. "My name is Tristan," he offered. "I have a sister, Isabella."

"I am Joseph," the Indian said, his voice deep and slow.

Tristan raised his hand in greeting. He felt like doing a cub-style handshake, but wasn't quite sure how that would go over. Joseph then led Tristan further into the cave. Four others joined them.

"Where are we?"

"This is our vestibule, our entry room," Joseph explained.

I gathered that, thought Tristan. "Entry to your home? Your world?"

"Ah, yes, I see what you mean. This is our home, and our world too." He made a wide gesture. "We live in this place."

Tristan glanced down at the bowl of blood. It reminded him of Peter's death. He nodded at the bowl. "Did you know Peter? Did he know you were here?"

All the Indians nodded slowly. Tristan realized the others were older, more solemn. Joseph hung his head. "He was our friend. He was a safe person. His great-grandmother had spoken to him through his mother. She had told her granddaughter many stories. Peter came to believe the stories. And when he came to live here it was because he wanted to know the truth."

"The truth," Tristan paused. "Where are we now? I jumped in the Blue Spring and now I'm here." He looked around.

"Yes, we are below the Blue Spring. Beside the Blue Spring, near the spring that feeds her. We're at the source. It's a place of sacred magic."

Tristan nodded and fell silent. In a way, if he didn't speak, he knew things. In the silence, he could hear. The room was cool and had a bluish glow. He observed the four Indians slowly gathering amongst themselves.

He simply waited. As he listened he heard sounds coming from his mind, or memory; not from this place. "We are here." He remembered those words from his parents. To hear, to be here. He went back and forth, hear, be here, hear—here. Are there no accidents in the English language? Are hearing and being here somehow related? His mind wandered and pondered in the silent noise of his thoughts, much like Alice in her fall down the rabbit hole. There was a kind of absurdity in the underworld. His thought was in the underwater. Underwater—underwater, he mused. He never thought of that before.

Perhaps the human mind only imagines under earth, but to conceive of depths beneath the deep, that was a new concept. Possibly, that's why the Indians had hidden successfully. The sound he'd been hearing he realized, was *Source* water; the water that fed the river. The light shone reddish now. A rosy light reflected from coral shells. It reflected sunlight and the blood in the bowl. The crystals were now purple amethysts, with the red infusing the blue, the whole place becoming purple. Whole—hole. Here he was in the whole world of a hole. A hole in a sense, a cavity, an absence of matter, yet a space sure enough—a tangible, full radiant purple place.

There's more place here in this space, he thought. A ringing ensued, a kind of clear ringing like a bell, a clear high bell. Was this a repetition of notes or just one note echoing back and forth endlessly from wall to wall? And then a new tone, low and sonorous, began to fill the space.

Shadows seemed to be moving in and out. He felt his forehead—his nose, his entire face was tingly. Kind of buzzing. He thought he should move, so he did—in the ringing, chiming, buzzing, tingling vibration. The air had become thick as water with all the sound and vibration. He saw Joseph up ahead. Calmly, without fear, he put one foot in front of the other and moved towards the figure with elated steps. He was enthused, excited, even ecstatic. Joseph kept moving further, so he followed. As he followed, he focused and refocused because the dimness kept giving way to bits of white light, which made him blink as if a strobe infused his brain. He wanted to shut his eyes, but he needed to follow the figure, the silhouetted form of Joseph, who led him out to the green world of grass and trees once more. The sun was low in the sky.

"Your vest!" exclaimed Tristan. "It's made of so many colors. Like the fish you caught for me. Oh I get it, like Joseph in the Bible with his many colored coat."

"Like whom?" Joseph looked long at Tristan.

"Oh you know, the Bible?" He asked. "Do you have school here? You speak English well, do you read books and all of that?"

"Of course," replied Joseph.

"This place looks similar, but different."

"It's the same place you were exploring in today, but further away, a little beyond where you normally go. You see with new eyes now. Do not be surprised. We frequent the more obscure parts of The Ranch, as you call it."

"How many of you are there?" Tristan asked.

"A lot. A whole tribe. My grandmother shall tell you our story later. How do you feel, by the way?"

"I feel wonderful. I feel great, I really do. Where are we going?"

"Follow me. It's late. You must return. In a moment we will emerge on the hill beside the Blue Spring. Your family will be glad to see you."

"That was a wonderful room," Tristan said.

"Now you know our secret." Joseph's brown eyes looked straight into Tristan's. "Please promise me you will return." Joseph held his gaze, "but you must guard the secret. That is essential."

"Yes of course, but how can I ever go back?" Tristan hesitated as he turned to go back to the others.

"You will find a way. That too is ordained." But at that moment Tristan did not realize how long it would be before he would return.

CHAPTER 24 *After the Fall*

Mariah panicked. First the Ranch had taken Peter's life, and now it had taken her son as well. She tore her hair and searched the sky for answers.

Then she saw it—a speck, just a shimmer of light in the distance. She squinted into the setting sun. There in the distance was Tristan's small figure. He stood so still. Sopping wet in the evening light.

"I'm cold, mama."

She ran to him. Stumbling on stones in her rush. Sobs and tears wet her smile. She grabbed him up in her arms. He's alive and real. Relief and exhaustion caused her to squeeze too tight as she hugged him to her and tried to warm him. "Yes, I bet you are honey."

"I'm fine, really," Tristan laughed and regained his footing.

David picked up Isabella and ran to them. As they stood sobbing and hugging, tears streaming, there was a rustle in the woods behind them. Mariah turned to see a black creature come bounding out to great them, tail wagging. The shiny black Labrador, with its paws splashing in the shallow stream, trotted up to join them. Mariah felt the sand paper tongue on her hand as she extended it in greeting. Tristan patted the dog's head.

Mariah looked up hard at David. "Is this? It can't be. Is this Peter's dog, Samson?"

"I think it is," David said. "C'mon, It'll be dark soon. We better get a move on." He spoke firmly to hide the sheer relief of finding his son.

Tristan took his mom's hand. She felt like he was comforting her more than seeking it. So grown up and like a child too. They looked down at the now dark, cold water. Once the sun sunk behind the hill the water grew dark and ominous. She shivered. Isabella held David's hand and Tristan held his mother's. They made their way down the hill around the steep grade that plunged down into the Blue Spring. They hiked in silence. When they finally reached the bottom they had the long trek back to the campsite in front of them. The twilight lit the silvery maples and the sky slipped into darker hues of blue as the sun sank. The Dog obediently joined them on the trek.

"It's late, isn't it David?"

"Yes, honey." Silence followed the crunch of their footsteps along the path. The children were quiet as they followed the familiar path along the river and through the clearings hedged with small cedar trees. An occasional bird flew out from hiding, startling them.

"Tristan, son, are you sure you're all right?" David said, "You look good, but is everything OK?"

"I'm fine, but I am not ready to talk about it yet. It would be awesome to spend the night around a huge warm fire."

"I think we can handle that," David spoke with false cheer.

Tristan bonded with the dog on the long hike. David lifted Isabella up on his shoulders when she grew sleepy.

Mariah was silent as she tried to understand what had happened. He had jumped into the Blue Spring pool, but they had found him walking along the trail. Mariah recited the entire passage about Children from 'The Prophet,' "Your children are the sons and daughters of life's longing for itself. They came through you but not from you...You are the bows from which your children as living arrows are sent forth. The Archer sees the mark upon the path of the infinite, and he bends you with His might that His arrows may go swift and far." Hard to do, easy to say, she realized in acquiescence to all parents everywhere.

Mariah stayed beside her son as they strolled along Jade Cove

Lake. This river is quiet and hushed. Still, in a way that draws me in, she thought as she stared down at the green velvet dark depths. She knew this river of her present reality was awesome in its cold depth. She pondered the mysteries that lay hidden below the surface. The persona evident here, was so different from her own. She thought the river of her own imagination sparkled like diamonds, and shimmers, laughing over rocks and splintered stone.

She hugged her boy closer, knowing the door had closed for a time and the coldness held secrets she may never know. The family hurried, to race the solid black night. Regardless, it settled upon them, before they could find the car.

"David, I think it's our time to go." Was The Ranch pushing her away now? Had their happy trespass, though brief, offended the River God?

"Can we keep the dog? Who's feeding it?" Tristan asked.

"Someone's caring for it. Look at how healthy and shiny he is," Mariah said.

By the time they found the car, there was an eerie silence everywhere.

"With Peter gone we are sort of trespassing. I don't feel safe anymore." Mariah spoke in the eerie stillness.

They all turned. The dog had vanished. Mariah got chill bumps all over her arms. One minute it had been there, running to and fro with Tristan, distracting everyone from the near tragedy.

"Samson, here boy," Tristan's voice sounded loud. Then it was swallowed by the dead silence all around the meadow. The circle of woods stood like a silent sentinel at attention, all secrets melting into the twilight.

They all ran to the Volvo and jumped in. David was thankful they had a sturdy, solid vehicle. He fumbled in his pockets for some keys. He put them in the ignition. It wouldn't start.

"It always starts," Mariah said.

They disembarked and looked around at the quiet field. A breeze gently waved the prairie grasses. They looked up at the midnight blue sky with the first stars twinkling above. Mariah and the kids held hands and said a prayer.

"Try it again," Mariah said.

This time it worked. They jumped back into the car to escape.

"Another adventure," beamed Mariah. "Now we have to pray we make it safely out of here with no one noticing us."

"Like who?" asked Tristan. He was smiling and she could tell he didn't need an answer.

"I was saying, what a treasure to be greeted by Peter's dog." She could drop the debate about stealing a dog, after they had trespassed on the Ranch.

Everyone held their collective breaths; until after driving for miles through the interior, the last cattle gate banged shut behind them. David drove through the darkness, back to the highway, and away from The Ranch.

The following day, a hundred or more miles deep into West Texas, the family found an oasis in the desert complete with a campground and spring fed swimming pool. A couple of days here would be good they decided. No reason to push their luck any further at Peter's Ranch.

Mariah awoke abruptly from a deep dreamless sleep. David perched beside her sleeping bag, already dressed with a cup of coffee in his hand. She sat up on one elbow, squinting in the sunlight.

"Good morning, Sunshine." He called her by her nickname.

"Wow, I feel like I've been drugged. I slept hard. What time is it? Is Tristan up?"

"Early enough. Come on. Let's get some camp breakfast started."

"Good idea." She untangled her limbs from the sleeping bag.

Soon they sat sipping coffee with smoky tortillas and tasty Mexican eggs with lots of cheese. David watched Mariah thoughtfully.

"You're waiting," she observed. She studied his patient eyes under the fallen lock of hair and bit of scruff at his jaw line.

"And you are not talking for a change. Must be heavy." His words were light, his presence full of concern.

"I don't know if I should say anything yet. I'm thinking. How long are we going to stay out here? I get the feeling we won't be going back to Houston ever. We probably won't be eating nice American breakfasts like this very long either. We'll have to get creative."

"Tristan hasn't said a word all morning. He's off by himself, drawing."

The night before, when they had set up camp and gotten a good mesquite fire going, Tristan shared his adventure beneath the spring. It felt fine and safe to talk about it under the night sky. It sounded fantastic, like one of her father's stories, she mused. Mariah thought it may or may not be true. It was more fun to believe it was.

"I feel they have entrusted us with their secret. Like they trusted Peter," Mariah told David.

"You mean you believe Tristan's story."

"Of course I do. Where did he go? We all saw him jump in the water, and then we found him much later on the cliff beside the spring. Besides, how many people do you know like Peter?"

"None. Zero. Zilch."

"Right, that's what I was thinking. Or Tristan for that matter." They both sobered at the implications.

"David, thanks for being patient. I'll have to go back out there again." She met his eye so he knew she meant business.

"You're being obtuse. What's going on?"

"Tristan told me what happened again in full detail. He met the Indians in their sacred lair, or temple. He saw their world. I believe him."

"He's a child. A very adult child yes, but children have imaginations—especially bright ones. But still, Tristan seems

166

changed. I can see a change." He studied her face, Mariah's green eyes bright and serious. "Do you mean alone? You want to go back alone?"

"Yes. If the Indians let me in."

"Do you think they will?" His blue eyes opened wide. He knew this was a ridiculous conversation. One minute he didn't believe they existed; now he was discussing them.

"I think they come in dreams like in the teepee when I was younger. There is some connection." Mariah looked off, her thoughts bigger than she could verbalize. Like her dream that gave her foreknowledge of Peter's death. It was about Indian elders. They wanted to give her a gift, she mused. Foreseeing the future is a gift, but one she wasn't sure she wanted. She smiled at David, as he was still watching her, wondering whether she'd just gone crazy. "But first, let's you, me, and the kids have a normal fun day of play, swim, and sun at this amazing desert oasis."

David breathed a sigh of relief. "Good idea."

* * *

David thought about Mariah and her dreams. Nice symbolic messages. But Tristan had fallen into the water and was gone long enough to have drowned. Instead, he had emerged very much alive, but changed somehow. Now there were two mystics in the family. He would wait and see. He was an artist after all, not a skeptic.

"Penny for your thoughts?" Mariah glanced up at him with a curious smile. He smiled back but said nothing about what he was thinking. It was becoming more likely, he mused, that she already knew.

* * *

Over the next few years the Agnelli's took a lot of camping trips, but never again ventured to The Ranch. The magic world Tristan had discovered was left as a pristine memory. Tristan thought of the Indians often. The wonder of their world, replaced the horrid brutal reality of Peter's death. Knowing he had friends there, he dreamed of one day returning.

The family went on to New Mexico. They visited the Apache reservation in Ruidoso, arriving in time for the feast of the Maidens, held annually every fourth of July. Mariah sought advice from a wise Apache woman. She studied her face thoughtfully as she spoke, trying to keep Tristan's description of the Indian Brave he'd met beneathe the waterfall, in her mind, and compare it with the reality of the woman before her. She listened to stories of Geronimo, and his many years spent hiding in Arizona to avoid capture. The stories disturbed her. Real life was not as fantastic as the myths her imaginative children were concocting.

Face it, she was into fantasy. Something must be wrong with her, it had all seemed so real.

to be continued

"There is a way to live on the earth--a peaceful, gentle and harmonious way--and they know what it is."

Excerpt from the sequel: The Forgotten Tribe

"We have gathered now, in response to an intense weather forecast. All it takes is a few super-storms..."

"Storm surges and tectonic plate shifts," Jack interrupted, "and voilà, Tennessee is ocean front property. It seems Houston and La La land are both in severe danger of ocean proximity floods."

"Tectonic what?" Melanie asked.

"You know, in the city of angels," Jack offered. "Los Angeles has a fault line running through..."

"Later." Pat waved him off. She wasn't one to be thrown off course. "Last year was one of the worst hurricane seasons in history. The year Katrina was followed by Rita, the city was a disaster. We thought we would lose everything. Houston was impacted both physically and fiscally, and still hasn't recovered. Now, there are already ten of us who are planning to disappear—go into hiding, if you will—for as long as it takes this to pass."

There was silence, as people digested this.

"Wow," someone said.

Mariah was surprised. So this is what Jody and Pat had in mind? Go for it. Just leave. Mariah's thoughts raced, escaping her grasp like a bevy of helium balloons. She just didn't want to be here in the wet dismal floodwaters of Houston sewage. People died in this kind of storm. At sea level, intense rainfall quickly rose to dangerous flood levels. The storm sewers emptied into bayous, that once full, spilled their banks all over the streets, yards and houses. Even in a minor flood, damaged houses were ruined with black mold seeping into the sheetrock and wood floors. When they were kids, she remembered, they had once floated down the street in a rowboat rescuing animals. After Hurricane Rita hit Houston, anticipating hurricanes wasn't fun anymore.

"Of course, no one knows what is really going to happen, but we've been listening to the predictions for years." Pat was talking.

Mariah tuned back in to the grim reality they were now facing. She felt that buzz again. Her heart skipped. David and she had a game. If the dramatic picture of world collapse was really on the horizon, and they had to leave, who would they want to be stranded on that deserted island with? Their list of friends was growing. Jody knew all about the true history of North America and could regale you for days. Jack Java was enthralling with his endless stream of stories. Her new friend Hazel was full of wisdom and insights. Robin had a unique view of the world. Yes, she was prepared to leave the world as we know it, but only if her friends would join her.

Pat opened her mouth to speak, but instead they heard a male voice ring out from the other side of the room.

"Perhaps since we're already surrounded by government corruption, the earth is simply fighting back."

Mariah turned to see her old friend Paul; his long frame slouched against the doorjamb, black curls outlined his rugged features.

Pat started at the presence of this stranger. Then she noted his astute observation. "We don't know how or why, but the situation has become untenable. Most of you, I know, have developed your own income in jewelry, massage work, crafts, or healing arts, and are off the tax role. We are, after all, a small unit in a large universe. It may be easier than we think to disappear into the country."

Jody added, "Texas is one place that has vast amounts of unexplored territory. Much of New Mexico is reservation land. The question we put to you tonight is this: Are any of you prepared for this radical move? Are there any of you who care to join us?"

"I think," Paul added, "if things continue at this exponential rate of warming, we will all wind up living in caves below the earth's

170

surface. And we will only visit the surface in space suits as protection from the poisonous atmosphere we have created." An aquiline nose and dark brows put his intense gaze in shadow.

Pat's eyes flicked around the room as if to say, *who invited this guy?* "That's a very drastic picture of our future."

"Perhaps we should break up to discuss this. This will greatly impact all of our lives," Jody said.

The room was as silent as a tomb. No one had expected this, at least not so soon.

"Can't you feel it changing?
Hear the changes.
Surrounded by love,
In this one, beautiful, world."

from
The Forgotten Tribe

THE FORGOTTEN TRIBE, a novel
the sequel to *HEADWATERS*,
by Michelle Moraczewski
is now available on Amazon.com